Praise for

William P. Wood

"Wood clearly knows the inner workings of the judicial system."

—Publishers Weekly

"William P. Wood, a former prosecutor, knows well how to surprise and engross us."

—Vincent Bugliosi, author of *Helter Skelter*

"A natural storyteller!"

—Norman Katkov, author of *Blood and Orchids*

BROKEN TRUST

"Wood combines colorful, behind-the-scenes details with a nonstop plot."

—Library Journal

"A tour de force of compelling courtroom drama and spellbinding storytelling."

—Gus Lee, author of *No Physical Evidence*

"A spellbinding tale about the men and women who dispense justice from the bench."

—Associated Press

RAMPAGE

"One of the better courtroom dramas in years."

—New York Times Book Review

Also by William P. Wood

Sudden Impact

Broken Trust

Pressure Point

Stay of Execution

Rampage

Quicksand

Fugitive City

The Bone Garden

WILLIAM P. WOOD

THE BRIBE

A NOVEL

TURNER

Turner Publishing Company
4507 Charlotte Avenue • Suite 100 • Nashville, Tennessee 37209

www.turnerpublishing.com

THE BRIBE

Cover design: Taylor Reiman
Book design: Glen Edelstein

Library of Congress Control Number: 2014956031

ISBN: 978-1-62045-476-3 (paperback), 978-1-63026-749-0 (hardcover)

Printed in the United States of America

THE BRIBE

ONE

THIS GUY WOULDN'T SHUT UP.

Jamie Lorenz glanced back in the mirror at the passenger in his cab. There he was, looking out the window, talking a mile a minute and even laughing at his own jokes. Once again Jamie had the feeling he'd seen this guy some place before, the late-forties fleshy face with its brown and gray hair stuck flat almost like it was combed with butter. And the wicked scar running down from the guy's right eyebrow.

One thing, Jamie thought sourly, this is a guy who definitely likes to hear the sound of his own voice.

For the last twenty minutes, right after he got into the cab at Sacramento Metropolitan Airport, he started. "Goddamn, it's great to be home, you know that? You ever been away and you get home and you just start realizing what a dumb-ass move you made leaving your home and your people, your family?" And the guy just went on after that, never pausing or apparently expecting Jamie would answer. They were making good time on I-5 heading south toward midtown Sacramento, which is where the passenger wanted to end up. The city's new skyline rose in the distance. The early evening October sky was split with surprising streaks of almost iridescent blue sky among the lead-gray clouds. Rain coming tomorrow, the weather reports all said.

A long line of trucks heading to Los Angeles slowed traffic down to a crawl. Jamie felt his passenger lean forward and the guy's ripe boozy breath was almost on the back of his neck.

"See all those new houses?" The guy pointed at the frenzied building springing up along either side of I-5. "Couple hundred million bucks out there right where I used to pop jackrabbits and gig for frogs. You ever think there's that much money on some muddy, stinking farmland? I sure as hell didn't." Then he was off about how his family had owned three hundred acres, sold it before the land was worth so much. And then how all of his buddies, the smart ones who were investors and developers, got rich buying up the land and holding it for fifteen years until the city exploded outward with so many people who came begging to them.

Jamie cracked his window to get some fresh air. Most of his passengers listened to him because he had a few things to say, about the Kings and whether they'd make the play-offs or about the courses he was taking at American River College in history. He was not going to drive a cab for much longer, and most of his passengers liked to hear him talk about the liquor store he was going to buy.

He frowned. He managed to get in a word about his future plans, and the guy leaned forward again. "Hey, you just reminded me. Get off on Garden Highway. There's a liquor store in Natomas and I want to stop there. Can't show up empty-handed," and he laughed at something funny in what he'd said and started talking about how people thought they knew other people but nobody had a goddamn clue about anybody.

Jamie turned off Garden, looping past Discovery Park and the wild tangle of vines and trees along the river. He followed the guy's jabbing finger into the Bel-Air Shopping Center and put the cab in neutral while the guy jumped out at the liquor store. He came back after about three minutes with a brown paper bag. "Okay, let's get this parade moving," he said, and gave Jamie the exact address.

Twilight was coming on quickly, the cool fall darkness that descends utterly in California's capital. Jamie was glad he only had a couple of miles to carry this guy. He figured he'd dump him out and circle back to the Hyatt's cab line and see what was going on. Tuesday like this, there were usually a couple of conventions in town and plenty of fares.

The address in midtown was one of the new lofts that had been carved from old auto dealerships or offices and then sold to wealthy retirees who liked the growing excitement of midtown or the younger hustlers who worked the legislature. Jamie was surprised. He hadn't figured his talkative, graying passenger for this high-priced, showy real estate.

He pulled up, got out, the guy already standing by the cab's trunk cradling his brown bag and gently rocking it in the crook of his arm. Jamie noticed that the animation had gone out of the guy's face and he was stone silent suddenly, looking up at the lights of the lofts on the second story. He started whistling a sad tune. A strong breeze rustled through the numberless oaks and elms along the street. A few cars, lights on now, rushed by.

Jamie hauled out the two battered but expensive leather suitcases, the kind you rarely saw anymore. "That's forty-two even," he told his passenger, but the guy already had a hundred out. Jamie took it, trying to figure the change when the guy's sad whistling broke off.

"Jesus!" he heard the guy shout.

Jamie's head snapped up just as the first shots broke the early night. He dropped some bills, and put his hands in front of his face, vainly trying to protect himself.

TWO

"I HATE HOSPITALS," Detective Terry Nye said to his partner, Rose Tafoya, as they pushed through the entrance to Sutter General's Trauma Center.

"Nobody likes them, Ter," she said. "You afraid somebody's going to give you a shot?"

"I just hate them," he said sourly, but Rose did make his days brighter somehow. They had been partners for almost a year and a half and Nye was pleased with that. They did not get on each other's nerves over the long shifts or the even longer cases. He no longer felt the inner chill that had been growing for years, and that change was entirely due to Rosie. She was just over thirty, athletic, she wore her black hair clipped and straight and she always dressed with keen attention to how professional she appeared. Like she could walk right into a courtroom or greet the chief of police.

"No, seriously, Ter," she said, hanging on as she always did when she knew she'd gotten to him, "what's the big beef with hospitals?"

4

"Okay," he said, as they rounded a corner through a set of glass doors and into the half-filled waiting room. "Way back, I'm the training officer for a rookie. We get called out in the middle of the night to Broadway. It's a weekend. We find this guy and his wife whaling away on each other in the middle of Broadway. We go in to break them up."

He went on as they passed families framing sick kids, a black man and his girlfriend doubled over, and assorted others sitting forlornly in the bright fluorescently lit room waiting for their numbers to be called. Rose gave a sympathetic look to a woman holding a small girl with dark-circled eyes. Her own daughter was now ten.

Nye said, "But then the guy, mope husband or boyfriend, I forget, he gets my rookie's baton away and then the woman, she jumps on my back and starts whacking on me." His voice filled with remembered indignation. "And the rookie's trying to pull her off me and we got these cars going by all around us, honking like crazy."

Rose smiled. "Dancing the night away."

"Yeah. So then the guy lets me have it right over the ear and just opens me up like a tomato. I'm bleeding like a son of a bitch and my rookie's screaming like hell and it was one big great messed-up bust."

"Hospitals, Ter? Your deal with hospitals?" she prompted.

"So I get hauled to this joint." He waved his hand around. "Only it ain't as neat and modern, and some donkey just out of med school sews my head like he's making a quilt." He lowered his head and pushed the gray hair away over his right ear. "Looks like the goddamn San Andreas Fault," he said, showing her the jagged scar. "So that, Rosie, is the reason I hate hospitals."

She nodded. "Okay. Tell me who the rook was."

Nye shook his head. "I ain't giving anybody up."

"It's got to be somebody I know," she prodded.

"All I'm saying is that this rookie's gone on to bigger and better things in the department and every Christmas I get a family-size bottle of Scotch. Which was nice when the wife and I were drinking the stuff." He meant before his noisy, bitter divorce.

"That's a bribe," she said, grinning.

"All depends on how you look at it." He shook a finger in the air.

They waded into a half-dozen uniformed Sacramento Police Department officers grouped around the main doors to the emergency rooms. Nurses and doctors milled at the doors, some darting away, others arriving. The detectives went through the doors.

Rose said quietly, "This is a party. You hear anything else about the call?"

"Just what you did. Two down. Shooting in midtown. Transported to Sutter General."

"Too many folks, Ter," she said, noting the collection of cops and medical staff. There was an unknown element to the radio call they had received ten minutes earlier, and they both knew it was about to reveal itself in all of its unpleasant glory.

The emergency rooms were either cubicles or partitioned areas with beds and equipment jammed into them. Nye saw that only one of the partitioned areas was occupied, and around it on the floor were bloody sponges and gloves, on the walls were spatters of blood, the complicated machinery silent, the whole sad testament to a life-and-death battle fought and lost. Medical orderlies were gathering up the debris, starting to mop down the wet floor. Four men and women, along with rumpled and red-stained doctors, were grouped beside the covered form on the bed. They were talking loudly over each other.

One of the men turned to Nye and Tafoya. He was in his early fifties—aged, broad, dark-haired, and his smile seemed like a half frown. "Detectives. It's good to see you."

"Mr. Cooper," Rose said formally. Both she and Nye had worked with Dennis Cooper, the senior deputy district attorney in Sacramento County, on a number of very high-profile homicides in the last few months. There was some quality about Cooper that resisted familiarity. Particularly tonight, Rose wouldn't have called Cooper by his first name.

Nye nodded. "What's going on?"

Cooper pointed to his left. "I don't think you know Alfred Walker. He's the new special agent in charge for the bureau."

Nye and Rose shook hands quickly with the solidly built younger man. He had a neat brown moustache. "Call me Alfie," he offered. "I brought some of my team." He gestured at the solemn men and women nearest him. Nye recognized two of them from past investigations. They looked back at him coolly. Working cases with the FBI was always tense and had been more so lately. The Sacramento office of the FBI had gone through four SACs in the last four years. Nye wondered if this latest one would last any longer than his politically tone-deaf predecessors, all of whom had stumbled badly over things they had done or not done about the California Legislature.

Cooper motioned Nye and Tafoya to the head of the bed. The doctors and the FBI had started heatedly talking to each other again. "Ladies and gentlemen," Cooper said, "let's hold it down."

They quieted, but only for a brief truce over whatever they were bickering about, Nye thought.

"Take a look," Cooper said, pulling down the sheet splotched with blood from the head of the body. He folded it back carefully, like he was tucking a child in for the night.

Rose peered at the white face, the nose startlingly and unnaturally sharp. The scar that ran down from one eye. When she looked up, she caught Alfie Walker and Cooper watching her, like it was a test. She shrugged and was about to say something.

Terry Nye said loudly with surprise, "Hey, I voted for this guy."

THREE

THEY MOVED PURPOSEFULLY from the emergency room to a conference room the hospital opened for them down the corridor. Cooper and Walker went ahead, the FBI agents bunched behind them. Nye and Rose followed.

She looked at Terry. His face was inscrutable. This one was going to be hard, very public, and a turf battle every step of the way with the feds. They both knew how the investigation would be played.

Cooper dropped his plain overcoat into a chair. "Sit down, everyone. We're going to have to engage our combined resources very quickly."

Nye muttered to Rose, "This is already starting to feel like the time I got the sixty stitches here."

"Should've sewed up your big mouth. I want to find out what's coming at us." But Rose was uneasy she hadn't recognized the victim. It was as if important, plainly apparent daily currents that affected her were obscure. She felt ignorant and it was an unaccustomed and unwelcome sensation.

Cooper glanced out the long windows at the fall night and the city's brilliant lights speckling it. "I'll start with what we know at the moment and then Agent Walker will describe the investigation task force we're going to create tonight."

The men and women waited. The FBI agents all had their legal pads out on the burnished brown conference table. Rose had her Palm Pilot and Nye his small notepad. Someone had left a tray of paper coffee cups on the table.

"Victim number one," Cooper said, "is Representative Gerald Booker. His district covers this county and two others. He's been in Congress five terms."

Walker broke in, "How many of you heard the congressman's speech in Washington yesterday?"

Nye sourly counted every FBI agent's hand raised. "I saw the headline in the *LA Times* today. That count?"

Walker ignored him. "Booker gave a speech in the House yesterday blasting corruption in Washington and saying that Congress was drowning in bribes, gifts, and payoffs." He threw a copy of the *New York Times* on the table. The banner headline was black and blunt, WAR HERO SLAMS CONGRESS. Below it, REP. JERRY BOOKER DECLARES, "THE DAY OF RECKONING IS HERE." Walker pointed. "That's the *New York Times*. It made headlines in every major paper and it led the news on CNN, Fox, and the networks last night."

"Yeah?" Nye said. "Where we going with the current affairs quiz?"

Cooper answered, "I think what Agent Walker is raising here is the significant possibility we've got an assassination on our hands."

"If we do," Walker added, "then all of us, state and federal, better get it wrapped up fast. We better have the answers."

"The simple reason is that if we don't, the questions that will be asked might take us all in directions none of us want to go."

Nye whispered to Rose, "I can see it. Lots of civilians, panic, lots of stop and frisk, dragnets. Yeah, that could be a problem."

The briefing was direct and simple. It was clear to Nye and Rose that no one knew much about what happened. Cooper read from a printout. "We have two victims. Victim number two is Jamie Lorenz, cabdriver, dead at the scene. Both he and the congressman were shot with the same weapon, it appears, a large-caliber handgun. Two shots to Mr. Booker, one to the torso, the other to his left arm. There was some hope he could be saved, but he died here about twenty minutes ago during emergency surgery. The autopsy will give us a bullet, with luck. With luck we'll also get something from it."

"Where did they get killed?" Rose asked.

"Outside on the sidewalk in front of 1820 N Street."

"Where'd the cab pick Booker up?" Nye asked.

"You'll have to find out."

"Why the stop on N Street?" one of Walker's agents asked.

"That's another one you'll have to find out."

Walker said, "We know Booker wasn't coming to see his wife. The family lives out in Carmichael."

"So who lives at 1820 N?" Nye wondered.

"You're going to have to tell us pretty fast." Cooper allowed a small grin. "We have questions and that's about all. Congressman Booker was in Washington, D.C., yesterday making a very newsworthy speech. He shows up in our city less than twenty hours later, and that means he probably took a red-eye. Who knew about it? Who knew he was coming here? Why did he come back here? Why was he miles from his home when he was killed?"

"And most of all," Walker said grimly, "did he get shot because of his speech?"

Rose turned to Nye. "You knew this guy?" she asked, low.

"Yeah, a little. Nailed him on a DUI twenty years ago. I'll tell you about it later."

Cooper was frowning at them. "I've spoken to Chief Gutierrez already and he's giving us a conference room on the third floor. He's assigning both of you"—he pointed at Nye and Rose—"along with three other members of the Major Crime Section, to this investigation. You're off regular rotation until we're finished."

"The bureau's putting my team in as well," Walker said. "And we've agreed to the generous offer to use the facilities of the police department."

The four agents looked vaguely ticked off, Nye thought. They liked people coming to them.

"Which brings us to the critical point." Cooper folded his arms. "The FBI will be the lead investigating agency in this case. The murder of a member of Congress is a federal crime. We also have a local civilian killed and that means Sacramento County has to be the other half of this investigation."

Rose whispered to Nye, "I think our half is the one that gets shit on if something goes bad."

"You think?" Nye answered.

Walker looked at his watch. "It's six now. What do you say, Dennis? Get everybody on the move, regroup at eight, then tomorrow at seven?"

"Fair enough." Cooper was politely distant. "Agent Walker and I've also agreed that Tafoya and Nye will be joined by Agent Zilaff." He pointed at a stocky sandy-haired man in a dark blue suit. "And the other team of Sacramento detectives will be joined with Agent Yang." The stolid woman nodded very slightly.

"You two," Walker said to the remaining agents, "get on the first plane back to D.C. and start working back through Booker's Capitol office. Everybody gets a top-to-bottom eyeball and I want every piece of paper in that office so you'll have to get a judge to give you a warrant because every move we make is going to be rock solid when we go into a courtroom."

"I admire your optimism, Agent Walker," Cooper said with an empty smile.

"Count on it, Dennis. We will bring down the shooter."

"I don't doubt it." Cooper sounded less than entirely convinced. "I know it goes without saying, but there is a complete media embargo on everything connected to this investigation. Agent Walker, Chief Gutierrez, and I will be holding a press conference in an hour. No one should say anything to the media before clearing it with either of us."

"So what do you want us to do?" Nye raised his hand sarcastically.

The men and women got up, coats pulled on, murmuring to each other.

Cooper bent and got his own overcoat. "Detective, you and your partner and Agent Zilaff will go see Booker's family immediately. I don't think this will hold until our press conference. I'd rather his wife hear it from you."

Nye got on his overcoat and helped Rose with hers. It was a small routine and he hadn't been sure she would even expect him to do it, but she realized he liked doing it. They spent a moment talking with the FBI agents, all of them now formally bound together on an investigation like many others in terms of procedure and protocol, but also like many others whose outcome was unknown. It was, Nye told Rose soon after they had become partners, like sticking your arm up the chimney to clean it, a chore he hated as a kid. You never knew what was up there. "Santa don't come down very often," he told her. "If you're lucky, it's soot and dead leaves. But maybe it's something that wants to bite your damn arm off."

Walker started out of the room with his other agents, and Cooper came up to Nye. "Terry, after you talk to Mrs. Booker, I want you and Rose and your new best friend to go out to the scene. Take a look. Tell me what you think. I don't see how I can get over there any time soon."

"Sure. You think you won't get everything straight from your new best friends?"

"I prefer to hear what you and Rose glean there."

Nye realized Cooper was adding a layer of protection for all of them in case there was a problem later on with the FBI, making sure that Sacramento detectives provided an independent assessment of the shootings. "What about checking the building? We got guys doing a canvass?"

"As we speak. But you better get moving. Right now, all the media knows is that there was a shooting. They don't know who the victim is." He caught up with Walker.

Rose finished shaking hands with Zilaff as they left. Nye

stuck out his hand. Zilaff had a dry, meaty grip.

"Come on, Zilaff," Nye said, "we should be real happy. Lot of times it takes a whole case to figure out where you are on the team roster."

"Where are we?" Zilaff asked.

Rose rolled her eyes because she had, by now, heard almost all of Nye's favorite captions about life and their job.

"We're the second-string towel guys, and girl, the mopes who pick up the towels after the team's done."

Zilaff grimaced. "I played football in college. I remember after a game."

Rose made a dismissive gesture. "Don't listen to him. He stopped drinking a couple of years ago and he's just a dirty, nasty, sour old man."

"I don't think many of those are in my favor, Rosie."

"I'll flip you both to see who tells Booker's wife," Zilaff said.

"Oh, you're going to be just fine," Nye said. "Rosie'll drive."

In the parking lot, Cooper saw the TV satellite trucks coming in. The illusion of having real control over this investigation was fading swiftly. Once the stories started, the speculation about why Booker and the cabdriver Lorenz were killed would flare, spread, and feed on itself even if there was nothing else to keep it burning wildly.

"Some people are afraid of reporters," Walker said. "I'm not. You have to know what they need, what they expect, and let them have it. Then they're on your side."

"I'd be interested in learning how you do it. I haven't found most reporters that predictable," Cooper said. The siren of an ambulance cut off abruptly as it braked to a stop at the trauma center and nurses and a doctor came running to meet it. "I've got to give the district attorney another update. She's in Sarasota, Florida. Her mother's dying. She can't get back here."

"Then you're in charge."

"Probably so."

"The ground rules between you and me." Walker gestured. "We're clear? I think you've got a great start, great attitude. The one thing"—he leaned closer because there were people in the parking lot, reporters and their camera crews piling out of the trucks—"is complete honesty, Dennis. Sometimes these interagency investigations can get ugly. I'm going to tell you whatever I've got. I'm going to expect you'll tell me the same."

"We're not going to get anywhere if we do anything else." They stopped at their cars, parked side by side. The reporters were hurrying into Sutter General. "If this was a political killing, I can imagine what Congress might do. Before we can think it through or see where it all leads."

"These are scary times. We have to keep moving ahead faster on this one."

"The first thing we better do, then, Alfie, is put your agency to work providing all the information they can gather about Booker."

Walker got into his car, snapping on the headlights. "Done. I've had stacks of files on Booker for a long time. It's amazing stuff. I'm having it sent out electronically now. I should have most of it for you by the eight o'clock briefing."

"What have you got?" Cooper asked, startled by Walker's revelation.

"See for yourself, Dennis. I don't want to spoil the surprise. Meet you at the PD." He wheeled his dark government car out of the parking lot.

Cooper got into his own car. After twenty-three years as a deputy district attorney, rising from doing disturbing-the-peace cases to complex homicide trials, he had found that the one invariant rule for a prosecutor was that surprises were rarely good.

He started the car, reached for his cell phone to call Sacramento County District Attorney Joyce Gutherie and tell her that one gigantic surprise about a murdered congressman, and her personal friend, was about to jump out from its hiding place.

FOUR

THE FIRST THING COPS, whether state or federal, from the smallest town to the biggest law enforcement agency in the world, did when they met was to determine, as fast as they could, who they knew in common and could agree was a lousy peace officer.

Rose drove the three of them to Carmichael, having gotten the address from Zilaff. Terry, beside her up front, and Zilaff in the backseat, were cycling through names and cases trying to find a connection. Over the course of his years with the SPD, Terry had worked with almost everyone. He could usually find somebody. But he hadn't had any luck with the dozen or so names he'd rattled off.

"You work with Borden over in Sheriff's Narcotics?"

"Don't think so."

"Ter, remember Noonan?"

"Which, the older one or the younger one?"

"The one who got his squad car stolen."

"That's Les, the older one." Nye twisted to look at Zilaff. "Noonan takes a break, gets a pizza or something, doesn't call

15

in, and his car gets swiped from the parking lot while he's inside doing a double cheese pepperoni."

Zilaff shook his head. "That's a note on your jacket," meaning the permanent personnel record that followed police officers throughout their career.

"Listen, the jackass did it again about two weeks later, and he got his car stolen a second time," Rose hooted. "He was in Auto Burg."

"Not for long," Zilaff said.

"Right. He left about a year later. Got a job in Arizona and probably got his car swiped there."

"Baton too, maybe," Rose jabbed.

"Do not," Nye said warningly. He turned back to the busy nighttime highway. "Come on, Rosie, I want to beat the nightly news." He was monitoring the civilian radio and the police computer on the dashboard for any sign that the story had broken about Booker's murder.

"Hold on. I'll use the toys," and she activated the siren and the flashing lights the car otherwise concealed behind the grillwork. The crush of commuters and truckers rapidly swung to the right and their car sped forward. "I'll knock them off when we get closer. I don't want to scare the family."

They were quiet for a moment, thinking about the horrific change they would soon bring about in the late congressman's family. Nothing could change what had happened, was the way Nye had put it to her after they visited their first victim's family, a bar beating that went too far. "Look, it's a mercy when we do it and they don't get it from neighbors or somebody screaming or crying. No matter what they call you, Rosie, and sometimes they act like you killed whoever it was, you're helping them."

She had tried to remember that advice when the accusations and obscenities flew at her or, worse, when the grief hardened a father, mother, or wife into a depthless silence.

"Hey, what about Andy Metzger?" Nye said to Zilaff. "He was around for a long time. He did that bank robbery deal in Citrus Heights with you guys, the guy who kept wearing a Dodgers cap?"

"Doesn't ring any bells."

"So how long you been part of Walker's team?" Nye laid unnecessary stress on the last word. He was frustrated that his encyclopedic knowledge of local law enforcement had proven useless.

"What time is it?" Zilaff pretended to look at his watch. "I got sent out here from Seattle day before yesterday. I met Alfie forty-eight hours ago and counting. I've been working on white-collar cases."

"Like what?" Rose asked.

"Scams at Boeing, problems with the books at a couple of aerospace companies around Seattle. My background's in accounting."

"This is your first homicide?" Nye asked with undue politeness, as if he was afraid of unnerving Zilaff.

"First one. Don't worry about me. If nothing else, I've got three kids and I'm pretty much ready for anything."

"Rose and I'll take this one," Nye said. "Okay, Rosie?"

They had been talking loudly over the siren, and when she suddenly switched it off and the lights, Nye's words were out-of-place shouts.

She nodded and Nye thought she was preoccupied about something. "We're about a block out, I think," she said.

Nye looked over the expensive, sprawling homes and carefully trimmed lawns as they went past. A few people were out walking or chatting with their neighbors, and a few kids on bikes rushed down the streets. Rose made another right turn and they were in a different neighborhood, the homes spread farther from each other, some with tall wrought-iron fences around them, or even elegant whitewashed walls.

"Got to be near here," Rose said, checking the numbers high up on driveway entry posts or on the bony white walls. "There we go. Straight ahead, Ter."

Nye studied the expansive three-story mansion as they drove up the short driveway. It was brightly lit up, cheery against the October night. Tall elms framed the front of the mansion, and in the four-car garage off to the left side, Nye spotted a Rolls Royce and a Jaguar. "I could afford maybe a couple of those tires," he said coolly.

"What's a place like this going for now?" Rose's cell phone buzzed raucously as they got out. She snatched it from her coat pocket.

"You're asking me? I been renting since the divorce. What's this worth up in your area, Zilaff?"

They walked to the front door, mock brass gaslights on either side. "Easily two or three million. Maybe five depending on what's inside."

Nye noticed that Rose was speaking harshly into her cell phone, her back to him. "Somebody living here's doing something right." He waited until she ended the call, and she joined him, her face set and angry. "Problems?"

"Sorry. I told Luis never to call when I'm working unless it's an emergency. He calls and says it's an emergency because he's tied up and he can't pick Annorina up after karate." Rose and her husband were growing more hostile every day, it seemed to Nye. "He said it was fine this morning and now he's all tied up with this stupid band and rehearsals and that's more important than our daughter."

"Zilaff and I can take care of this," Nye tried, knowing instantly what her reaction would be.

"Bullshit, Ter. I told Luis to go get her and bring her home and make sure she's got dinner, just like we worked out. He can't just change things because he feels like it." Rose's husband, after several years of deep reflection on what direction his life should take, had determined that he was a musician and had joined a fledgling garage band. That left Rose supporting the family entirely.

"You're okay now?"

"I'm great."

Nye glanced at Zilaff. "Rose'll take lead on questions, right?"

Zilaff nodded and Rose took a deep breath to steady herself for what was about to happen. Whoever lived in this grand, bright, and confident home would remember the next few minutes forever. The days and years would always be reckoned as the ones before the two detectives and the FBI agent arrived at the door and the ones afterward. The cleavage would be deep and irrevocable. Sometimes it was welcomed. Most of the time it was terrible and, on the worst occasions, lethal itself.

"Here we go," Nye said somberly as he rang the doorbell. A melodic chime sounded somewhere inside the house. They listened as they stood, a night breeze touching them.

The front door was opened by a tall woman with light gray hair, dressed in fashionable exercise sweats, holding a small towel to her face, breathing heavily. "Yes? What do you want?"

"Mrs. Booker?" Nye asked. He had his badge out. "We're from the Sacramento Police Department and this gentleman is from the Federal Bureau of Investigation."

She stopped dabbing her face. "This is something about Jerry."

"Yes. It is. Can we come in?"

"Joyce?" Cooper said loudly into his cell phone. "I can barely hear you."

"You're fine, Dennis," said the Sacramento district attorney from three thousand miles away. "I'm at the Orlando Airport waiting for my sister's plane."

Cooper thought he could hear faint announcements from a public address system. "Things aren't so good?"

"No. It's a matter of days."

"I'm sorry, Joyce." They had been friends for over a decade. There was talk in California's political circles from time to time that Joyce Gutherie would be a formidable candidate for attorney general. Cooper thought she was just ambitious and self-confident enough to entertain the talk without letting it become serious and turn into action. "I wanted to let you know where things are on the Booker investigation right now."

He gave her a short recounting of the meeting with the FBI and the activities that were under way at that moment.

"I can't leave, Dennis," Joyce Gutherie said.

"I can handle things. I don't know Walker, though. We had a meet and greet over coffee when he first got here."

"Keep him close."

"Thank you, Godfather." It was an old joke between them. Gutherie became more friendly and polite as she sensed a threat to herself or the DA's office. Cooper knew he ran to different reactions, combative, blunt, and tenacious. But he was trying to do a little of what had worked well for Joyce Gutherie in her career. "He says he's got files on Booker."

"What's in them?"

"I'll find out tonight."

There was a long pause and he thought she had broken the connection until the PA announcements started again.

"Jerry Booker was one of my first friends when I got to Sacramento. I told you about the time we met? It was a party downtown, a lot of younger, eager legislative staffers, a few courthouse lawyers to make it noisier, and Jerry. He was about the only air force or even military person there. I don't know who invited him. It was a couple of years before the Gulf War and his medals. He played the piano, he was funny. He was quite the life of the party." She paused again. "We got to talking and somehow I managed to pick up his cars keys from the kitchen table instead of my own. Neither of us should have been driving at that stage. We had a good time figuring that out when both of us couldn't think or see straight."

"I remember you told me."

"I am getting old."

"This was before he got married."

"Or I did. He supported me when I ran for DA and I had fundraisers for him when he ran for Congress. I haven't seen him or June for almost a year."

"Nye and Tafoya are out there now."

"This is so, so sad. I hear my sister's flight, Dennis. I want to know what Walker's got." Her voice was steely. "Let me know before anything's made public."

"I'll call you."

"I'm not saying anything stays hidden or covered up. I just

want to know. For myself. Along with everything else you're going to have to do, that's what I need from you."

"I promise, Joyce. Good luck to you and the family."

He ended the call. He had passed Sutter's Fort, still floodlit even though it was now closed for the day. It was a reminder of the fever time when gold glittered for the taking and avarice drew thousands of people from across the country. It was the true beginning of California's wealth and growth. In Sacramento over the years, when the names and faces changed in the old Governor's Mansion on Sixteenth Street or the legislature, it still seemed that the fever had never left, and all the many scandals and then reforms and new scandals arose from that primal glitter in 1849.

He didn't know what Walker had in his files on the dead Congressman Gerald Booker, but whatever it was had the power to taint and destroy many people because he had been such a public figure.

Cooper sped up down the tree-lined streets, passing old churches and new businesses. He briefly debated making a small detour to N Street to take a quick look at the crime scene himself, but realized he didn't have the time before the press conference.

One of the people squarely threatened by the FBI's files on Booker was his boss and friend, who waited on a deathwatch far away, powerless to do anything. He was going to have to make sure that justice was done in this case, all around, to the living and the dead. That was his burden.

As he went by Thirteenth Street he was at the edges of Capital Park, the verdant, densely tree-crowded area that surrounded the white-domed capitol itself. A short procession of men pushing shopping carts stuffed with black trash bags moved slowly up the sidewalk.

He called Leah Fisher, his assistant in Major Crimes, to tell her he was only a few minutes away and to find out what Walker was doing.

FIVE

JUNE BOOKER BROUGHT THEM inside the house into a high-ceilinged expensively furnished living room. A blue rubber mat and towels were laid on the floor in front of the television on which a silent energetic woman was frantically pumping her arms, the volume turned off.

Nye nodded to Rose. She would take the lead. The polished dark wood cabinets and tables, vases, and paintings scattered around the room were another visible reminder that the Bookers had a lot of money. He made a quick note in his pad to check on the tax returns, state and federal, of Booker and his wife. That was something the FBI could do very quickly. Maybe June Booker had money of her own. He didn't think Booker's air force or political careers added up to covering even a fraction of what he'd seen since they arrived.

June Booker listened as Rose told her the news about her husband. Zilaff's keen accountant's eyes swept the room. Bet he's got the price tag already, Nye thought.

"There's some mistake," June Booker said, sitting down on

a floral-print sofa. She looked puzzled more than anything else. "I spoke to Jerry last night. He said he wasn't coming home until the weekend at the earliest."

"There's no mistake, Mrs. Booker," Rose said calmly. "I'm very sorry."

"Please sit down. I feel like a terrible hostess." She motioned to them. Zilaff remained near the archway into the living room, while Rose and Nye took delicate antique chairs near the sofa. "You must be mistaken," she insisted.

"Your husband had his congressional identification on him, Mrs. Booker. Everyone at the hospital"—she paused, thinking, except me—"recognized him immediately."

"I don't know what to say," and there was suddenly a tremor in her voice even though she remained outwardly poised. Her hands clasped abruptly. "I mean, Jerry was very resolved about his speech yesterday when I talked to him. He said it was the right time and the right thing to lay out for the country. He said it was his wake-up call."

"What time did you talk to him, Mrs. Booker?" Rose asked.

"Last night at ten. Maybe it was eleven."

"So that would've been about one or two in the morning in Washington," Nye said.

"I didn't think about that." Her face was growing more rigid and her eyes fixed on either Rose or Nye with an intense coldness. "Jerry wanted to know how his speech had been covered here in California, who was commenting on it, who was calling. Some of our friends, people who'd contributed to his campaigns over the years, were confused and very upset. They didn't understand why he'd say what he did."

"We'll have to get a list of his campaign donors," Rose said.

"It's all public. Every donation is reported to the Fair Political Practices Commission and the Federal Election Commission."

Nye was interested in the questions June Booker wasn't asking. Like why her husband came to Sacramento unannounced or why he was downtown when he was killed.

"Mrs. Booker," he asked, sitting forward, "did your husband

have a meeting or business in midtown this evening, anything you can think of?"

"No. Jerry was staying in Washington, he said. He was going to make the rounds of the talk shows, and several reporters were coming in this morning. His speech had quite an impact. He was not coming back to Sacramento for a few days at least."

"But he did. So is there any reason you know of that could've put him on N Street tonight?"

"No. No. I can't think of any at all." She got up. She noticed the dervishlike exercise video trainer silently gyrating. "Vanity, I'm afraid. Watch what you eat, work out, remain serene." She stopped. "Well, it's all supposed to make you live longer and be happier." She turned off the television. "Another lie apparently."

"Is there someone we can call for you? Friend? Family?" Rose asked. She invariably made the routine offer, in these always extraordinary circumstances, sound sincere and concerned. Because she means it, Nye thought. Most of us, like me, just go through the motions most of the time. Not Rosie.

"My son and daughter are both in college, Colgate. I have to call them. I have to call the governor. I have to call the clerk of the House. They'll have to make arrangements. I have to make arrangements."

Nye saw she was drifting into that hazy territory that shock and grief opened up, where lists and mundane tasks futilely tried to delay the onslaught of the worst emotions, helplessness, emptiness, and loneliness.

Nye glanced around the room. It was, he thought, oddly laid out. Paintings and handsomely framed nature photographs all around but not one picture of anybody in the Booker family. So where were those pictures?

"Does your husband have an office here in the house?" Zilaff asked.

"Yes, I can show you," she said. Her rigid expression was dissolving. She started through the living room, leading them down a wide bright hallway, past a brighter kitchen. Nye glimpsed the shiny wide metal tables and a Hispanic woman busily chopping vegetables. She looked up curiously as they went by. "Tia's here so I'm not alone when Jerry's gone," June Booker said. "I should tell her to stop making dinner."

Zilaff trailed and Rose said, low, to Nye, "Something's out of line, Ter."

"No kidding. I don't what it is. But it is."

At the far end of the hallway, around a corner, June Booker led them into a spacious home office. It had four separate telephones, differently colored, two computers and fax machines, and a row of file cabinets. The furniture was functional but expensive. The walls of the office were covered solidly with framed photographs of Congressman Gerald Booker, much younger in an air force flight suit alongside a jet fighter, with his wife and then small children, and rank upon rank of him with two presidents, with senators and innumerable officials and an actor or two, speaking in a tuxedo at formal dinners, speaking from the back of a pickup truck, standing in the well on the floor of the House of Representatives, papers in one hand, mouth open. It almost made Nye dizzy, this overwhelming collection of self concentrated in one room.

He said very softly to Rose, "This guy couldn't turn his head without running into himself."

Zilaff was quietly appraising the equipment. Stacked on the floor were plaques and framed awards, and more photographs. There had clearly been no more room for everything to be hung. June Booker noticed him.

"We're still moving things around," she said, as if talking to homebuyers or old friends, "trying out where things work best. It seemed best to move all of Jerry's mementos into one place."

"How long have you lived here?" Nye asked.

"Almost eight months now."

"It's a very nice home," Rose said. "With your children in college, it must have been hard to buy this too."

"Jerry and I made some good investments over the years." June Booker folded her arms. "I have to call Gil Manzoni. He's Jerry's chief of staff. He's got to know."

"Back in Washington?" Nye asked.

"Gil's in the district office. It's on University Avenue. It's not far." She reached for one of the telephones. "He said he'd be working tonight."

"We'll let him know, Mrs. Booker," Nye gently moved between her and the phones. "What's the address?"

"One Thousand University Avenue," and as she spoke, Rose softly repeated it into her own cell phone so that an SPD officer could be dispatched to the address immediately. Nye knew what the instructions would be: Keep an eye on the place, make sure this guy Manzoni was there, and wait until the detectives showed up.

"Thank you," June Booker said. "Gil's almost part of our family. I can't imagine how he'll react. I can't believe it myself," and she started crying quietly. "Excuse me," and she turned back to the living room.

Nye didn't want her to be left alone for long. At this stage in an investigation, it was difficult to accurately determine what was going on. June Booker could be bereaved, overjoyed, suicidal, or homicidal. Nye didn't see the last two, but he wasn't going to take chances.

Nye said to Zilaff, "What do you want to do?"

"I want to keep an eye on all of this stuff." He pointed at the phones and the filing cabinets. "I want every piece of paper and every e-mail."

"Okay, Rose and I'll go meet the almost-part-of-the-family and see what he's been doing today."

"You're not going to touch anything?" Rose asked Zilaff.

"I'll wait for a warrant," he said. "I don't want to lose anything."

"Your curiosity's killing you, I bet," Nye said.

Zilaff grinned. "You have no idea."

Nye and Rose went back to the living room. June Booker sat at a burnished teak coffee table, and she stared ahead. "Mrs. Booker, we'd like to leave Agent Zilaff here with you in case you need anything. He can help."

"Oh. Yes." She looked at them. "I appreciate that. I was running through all of the people Jerry and I know. We send out six thousand Christmas cards every year, you know. I'm having a little trouble with who I should talk to at this moment. We have a lot of friends and a lot more acquaintances, but I really don't know who to talk to. Who do you tell something like this to anyway?"

"Your children," Rose said softly. "Take it one step at a time."

"I'd like to talk to Gil."

"Sure. Go ahead." Nye knew that there would be a cop right on top of Manzoni by the time she did.

He and Rose walked to the front door. June Booker stayed at the coffee table. As Nye pulled the front door closed behind him, he caught sight of her as she got up, went to the blue mat, and with fluid grace, did a handstand, holding it motionless in utter equipoise.

"Now I've seen it all," he said to Rose.

"It's just starting."

Four satellite TV trucks had rolled to a stop on the street outside the Booker mansion. The ominous drone of a TV helicopter and a bright white cone of light swept over the lawn, house, and driveway. Nye got on his cell to call for cops to come out and run the crowd control that would be necessary. Neighbors started spilling from homes farther up the street.

"Yeah," he said, sliding behind the wheel of their car, "let the show begin."

Rose radioed Cooper as they drove to let him know that Zilaff was sitting like a mother hen on a bushel of eggs and that a search warrant was required.

"We're about to go into the press conference with Chief Gutierrez and the US Attorney. I'll have Ms. Fisher work with Zilaff. I'll let Walker know we're going to state court for the warrant," Cooper said.

Rose could hear a loud babble of voices and sharp, irritated commands in the background. Someone yelled at a cameraman to stay back.

"That'll make him happy," Rose said sarcastically.

"It's faster than trying to get a federal warrant at this point. I've got two judges I can go to tonight. What does it look like we've got now?"

"Lots of records. Maybe Zilaff can go through them quicker than Ter and me. Congressman has a brand-new, very high-end house in Carmichael."

"What about his widow?"

"You hear that, Ter?" Rose asked Nye, turning up the radio's volume.

"Yeah, I heard. She's pretty tough. There's a funny feeling I get about her, the whole setup."

"She's got all of his pictures stuck in one room."

"Yeah," Nye said, "good example. All of his pictures so she don't have to look at them."

"Or him maybe."

Cooper said, "All right. I'll put Leah in touch with Zilaff and we'll see what the paper trail turns up. I've got to go. They're starting the press conference."

Rose finished with the radio. Nye had turned onto Fair Oaks Boulevard, passing across the aging steel bridge over the river, by a starkly modern Protestant church and then Cal State Sacramento to the right behind a stand of towering pines and evergreens. The office buildings along Fair Oaks were brick and Spanish colonial and home to insurance companies and physicians, medical labs. Rose knew that Sacramento might be officially the most diverse city in California, but in this section the faces were white. Almost exclusively. There were no ninety-nine-cent stores in the upscale shopping centers lined up on the boulevard.

"What're you worried about, Rosie?"

"I'm not worried. I'm thinking about Booker's widow."

"So?"

"There's trouble, Ter. She and this guy were not getting along. Seriously not getting along. She can't stand the sight of him."

"I got some of that, maybe not that much."

"Trust me. I know. Believe me, I do."

Nye looked at her for a moment. He wanted to help. "I was there before you. You're not the only expert." He knew Rose was brooding about her own difficulties at home and how to keep things together for her kid, maybe not for herself and her husband. He ached when she was troubled like this, and it had been ratcheting up for months now. Nye knew he couldn't even promise Rose things would be all right, that there would be a better time for Annorina and her at least.

There are promises that should never be made.

There are truths that no one gets to avoid. So he took a breath, said nothing, and turned right onto University Avenue. The pines were tall and concealing along the two lanes in either direction, giving the illusion of being far out in the countryside.

Rose shook her head. "Forget it. Look, tell me your DUI story about you and Booker."

"Okay, this is about twenty years ago. I'm like a nobody traffic cop, it's right after lunch." He stopped. "Hey, I'll finish later. We're here."

He swung into the nearly empty parking lot of a sandstone-fronted single-story office building. A single SPD patrol car was at the entrance.

"You pull this on me all the time. You start one of these war stories and then drop it," she said. "I'm going to get even."

"Yeah, yeah, yeah. I'm terrified." He unbuttoned his over-coat, looking up at the black, impenetrably clouded night sky. "One thing about the widow just now, I was figuring she had just about everything. I'm reconsidering."

They walked into the building, checking the directory and the room number of Congressman Booker's district office. "What else could she want? She's got that house, the cars, probably a lot more we're going to find out about."

Nye grinned. "She's calling the governor. She's calling the clerk back at the House of Representatives. Sad news. Hubby's dead. Nobody to represent the district in DC."

"You think she wants to go to Congress?"

"Wives succeed husbands in Congress, they retire, they drop dead, it's a solid fact. The governor calls a special election quick, and who has the edge? The lady with the name ID."

"Maybe she's got a reason to get rid of him."

"It's a good one. We better get the phone records for her for the last couple of days too, see when she and the congressman passed the time."

"Making a note." Rose tapped it into her Palm Pilot.

At the end of the hallway stood an SPD cop in a translucent raincoat. "You got some ID?"

"Cut it out," Nye said. "I'm Terry Nye. This is Rose Tafoya. The guy inside?"

The cop nodded. The Sacramento Police Department, with about three hundred sworn personnel and another three hundred civilian staff, was just large enough that patrol cops would not necessarily know detectives, even the ones in Robbery-Homicide. But no cop could mistake Nye for anything else.

"He's there. I said you guys were coming. He's gotten a couple of calls. I heard his cell. It plays that Beethoven thing," and he hummed the opening of the *Fifth Symphony.*

"'V for Victory,' they called back around your time, Ter." Rose smiled. "Old man."

"She's always trying to break my chops. Come on, let's try your stand-up routine on Manzoni," Nye said to Rose.

When they walked into the office's reception area, Nye heard the high-pitched whine coming from somewhere in the back. Booker's district office was a suite of three offices, two dark, the only light streaming from the back. He trotted forward anxiously. He knew that sound.

"More of him," Rose said, hurrying beside Nye, pointing at the rows of Booker's color photographs on the wall, campaign posters proclaiming A HERO FOR OUR TIME, and the framed adulatory newspaper endorsements. "These guys love themselves."

Nye only grunted. They got to the last office, the whine louder. A sandy-haired man in a white shirt, bright red suspenders, and a striped red, white, and blue tie was feeding papers into a waist-high machine that whined each time as if in pain, and turned the papers into a flurry of white snow falling in its transparent belly.

"Mr. Manzoni," Nye said sharply. "Hey. Manzoni."

The man raised his head, smiled, and pushed more papers into the shredder.

"Goddammit, cut that out," Nye said, pulling the machine's plug from the wall.

The aging police department's granite and iron building did not have a room large enough to accommodate the sudden deluge of reporters and camera crews that swarmed over it, as if spontaneously, when the media advisory about the shootings went out thirty minutes earlier. The news conference was moved three blocks away to the district attorney's office on G Street, just across from the sprawling white bulk of the Sacramento County Courthouse.

Cooper helped organize getting the reporters up to the third-floor conference room, and left it to the DA's small communications team to sort out where TV stations got their cameras placed around the room, and how to handle the podium now bristling with a forest of microphones in front of a blue curtain.

He moved everyone who was going to participate into Joyce Gutherie's office.

The US Attorney for the Eastern District of California, Iris Chang, was in deep and earnest conversation with Walker. Cooper looked at his watch again. The press conference was supposed to have started ten minutes ago, but Chang and Walker kept delaying it.

Cooper and Ed Gutierrez, the chief of police, waited in annoyance. "What the hell are they doing?" Gutierrez demanded. He was heavyset, with thick-rimmed glasses and a small salt-and-pepper mustache.

"Club Fed," Cooper said. "No outsiders admitted."

"Bullshit. I've got cops spread all over the city and I need to be back in my own office." He glared at Cooper. "This is our case. Booker and Lorenz go on my crime stats."

"I'll move them, Chief," Cooper said, heading for Chang and Walker. The noise from the reporters in the conference room adjacent to the DA's office was raucous, sharp, impatient.

Leah Fisher, blond, intelligent, and easily the most competitive member of his Major Crimes Bureau, intercepted him. "I've got Judge Roche standing by for our warrant. Zilaff's read me enough to put together the affidavit as soon as we're done with this. I'll take it to Roche's house."

Cooper sourly nodded. "They're plotting." He looked at Chang and Walker.

"Well, that's what they do."

She said it with such mock seriousness that he grinned in spite of himself. Leah had been a deputy district attorney for only eight years and she had reached the pinnacle of Major Crimes by hard work, keen judgment, and an indefinable quality of fairness and honesty that made juries trust her.

"I guess we can't count on dinner at home tonight," he said.

"Tonight was your night."

"I thought it was yours." But Cooper knew she was right. He frequently neglected his scheduled nights to make certain dinner was covered. Since he and Leah had moved into a rented house on Sutterville Road six months ago, there had been a myriad of things, large and small, to arrange like meals, her dog, their cars. He still had trouble believing it had worked out. Waking up in the early morning, seeing her face turned to him, her blond hair over one eye as she slept, struck him as almost unimaginable, and yet, he was lucky enough that it had happened. Only the constant undertone of office gossip about the two of them living together detracted from his happiness. Even Joyce was concerned, she told him, that morale among other deputy DAs was being affected. "It's none of their business," he bluntly retorted. "It's not yours either. Leah isn't getting any breaks or special treatment," which was the sharpest rebuke he had ever given his old friend.

"This is going to get out of hand, Coop," Leah said. "TV

and radio are putting out all kinds of rumors already. Middle East hit squads, death lists."

"It's time to apply a shot of rationality and cool things down."

He pushed by the other people in the room. The US Attorney and Walker stopped talking when they saw him.

"We've got to get started now," he said. "Rumors are flying. We've got to put the word out that this is an investigation like every other. We can't let panic or overreactions take over. The public needs to know that professionals are in charge."

Iris Chang, forty, lean and angular, in a beige suit and pearls, nodded very rapidly. "We're ready now. We're ready, right, Alfie?"

"I guess we are," Walker said, and Cooper caught his reluctance.

Something's going on, he thought.

He went to Leah. "Let's get our search warrant as soon as you can." He didn't add that it could at least be one part of the growing investigation they could use to bargain with the feds, if the need came up.

He walked into the blazing lights and shouts in the conference room with Ed Gutierrez. "This is when I would love being a patrol cop again," the chief said, squinting.

SIX

COOPER COUNTED TWENTY CAMERAS and lights crammed into the conference room, reporters crushed shoulder to shoulder, sitting on the floor all around the podium bracketed with United States and California flags, waving microphones and tape recorders like magic wands.

He introduced Chang, Walker, Gutierrez, and himself.

The room quieted and if he closed his eyes, it was possible to imagine it was empty.

"Tonight a major joint state and federal investigation is under way," Cooper said, "into the shooting this evening here in Sacramento of Congressman Gerald Booker and Jaime Lorenz, a driver with Yellow Cab. The shootings took place at approximately five thirty in the midtown area of the city. We are working on a variety of investigative avenues now, but the work is just beginning. We will be holding regular briefings for the media over the next twenty-four hours. It is vitally important to this investigation and to ensure public calm that any speculation about what occurred is completely premature and counterproductive. Let's see the evidence first."

He was about to turn to Iris Chang when a tall woman reporter beside her camera shouted, "Was this a robbery?"

"We don't know. We're checking everything."

"Was anything taken from Representative Booker or the cabdriver?"

"I can't comment on the state of the evidence."

Another reporter called out, "Mr. Booker gave a very controversial speech yesterday. Was he killed because of it?"

"There is no evidence of that at this point."

"How about a terrorist hit? There's a story on the wires that Booker was on a list of targets for assassination and the CIA's had the list for months."

The reporters broke into shouted, bellowed questions that overlapped into noisy incoherence.

Before Cooper could answer, the US Attorney pushed by him at the podium. Walker fell into place beside her, moving Cooper effectively to one side with Chief Gutierrez.

"Quiet, please, all right? Quiet. We do have some additional information," she said, and Cooper watched her with growing unease. Walker stared ahead.

"I have just spoken with the attorney general. He has instructed the Department of Justice that this investigation is to have the highest priority. He is in communication with other members of Congress, especially the leadership of both parties, to make sure that precautions are taken for their safety until we know exactly"—she glanced at Cooper and Gutierrez—"what happened tonight."

"Are they going to an undisclosed location?" someone snidely yelled out, but no one chuckled.

That isn't so bad, Cooper thought. The feds are only being careful.

He saw that Chang gripped the sides of the podium so tightly it looked like she was going to lift it over her head.

"Because Representative Booker held several distinguished awards from his flight duty in the air force during the Gulf War," she went on, "and because he was the ranking member on the House Aerospace and Military Appropriations Committees, the attorney general has directed that his murder will be treated as an act of terrorism. It may be domestic or foreign," and her final words, "until contrary evidence is uncovered," were drowned out in the explosion of hoarsely cried questions and the reporters all seemed to lunge forward as a single, frenzied mass.

Oh, dear God, Cooper thought in cold fury.

"You've been within ten feet of me for the last half hour and you could've given me some warning that she was going to throw a tanker truck of gasoline on this thing," Cooper snapped at Walker. "Jesus Christ, what are you people trying to do?"

"The AG is my boss. I play it his way."

"Every damn reporter is outside now telling the country, no, dammit, telling the whole world that Booker was killed because he's a war hero and he votes on defense budgets. He was targeted."

"I do not know that isn't what happened." Walker stood beside Cooper's desk. Cooper faced him, braced on his hands, white with anger. "It's the smart thing to start off with the worst possibility and eliminate it if you can. But it's also the right thing."

"Bullshit, as my friend Chief Gutierrez likes to say. You and Chang and the attorney general are going to stampede this country into paranoia before we even know what evidence we've got."

"Listen, Cooper, a dead congressman, a dead *war hero congressman* isn't the same thing as one of the ordinary chumps you handle every day, shooting at a liquor store, shooting at a bar, shooting over a car, a girl, a piece of burnt toast. This is much bigger."

"Right this minute, we don't even know if both Booker and Lorenz were shot because some *chump* wanted Lorenz's cash. We had two cabdrivers held up last month. It's conceivable," he snapped again.

"Then we'll find out if Booker or the cabbie was the target."

"Who's going to believe us now if it was all about the cabdriver?"

Cooper sat down, furious and frustrated. Chang had left the press conference, trailed by most of the reporters, when she ended by dramatically announcing that she was being called to Washington for immediate consultations with the attorney general and the White House. Gutierrez had stormed back to the police department, leaving Cooper to pull Walker into his office.

Cooper shook his head. "This is a hell of a way to start working together, Agent Walker."

"We've all got troubles tonight," Walker said. "I've got twenty agents flying in from a couple of states, Main Justice in Washington calling the plays. So what happens tonight and tomorrow, well, that's probably my career."

"That's no excuse," Cooper said. He got up. "You said we had to have honesty between us. I don't see how that's possible now."

For a moment, Cooper detected a struggle on Walker's face, as if he wanted to say something. They had been arguing earlier, him and Chang, and he lost, Cooper realized. Years of watching witnesses and jurors had attuned him to subtle shifts of expression. He didn't always get it right, but he knew at least when someone had more on his mind.

"We're going to have to make the best of things, Cooper. The AG wants us to nail Booker's shooter. Us. Not you."

"I don't want to turn this investigation into a race." But I sure as hell will if that's the only way to get the truth, he thought.

"It's not a race. You lose automatically. We've got more resources. We've got more reasons. Booker was a federal official." He turned to the door. "We've got our first sit rep meeting with our teams in about an hour. I'll make it official. FBI tracks Booker's leads. Locals follow the cabbie."

"We'll be running into each other every step of the way," Cooper said angrily.

"You better stay out of my way, then."

He didn't want Walker going back on any other pledges.

"Bring those files you told me about on Booker to the meeting, Agent Walker. I want to see everything."

Walker muttered "Shit" to himself and left.

For a moment, Cooper debated what to do next. His cluttered office, stacked with boxes of current death-penalty cases, bookshelves crammed with dog-eared state appellate court decisions, a few awards hanging on the walls from over the years, including Prosecutor of the Year from the California District Attorneys Association, mocked him silently. The feds could roll right over him, SPD, the whole state if they wanted to.

And Chang and Walker had made it plain that's exactly what they intended to do. The credit for resolving Booker's shooting would go to the feds.

Cooper got up, knowing what he had to do. He headed down the hallway. It was unusually busy tonight, the lights on in nearly every office, people talking, phones ringing. Somber faces passed him. Nobody sleeps tonight, he thought.

What ate at him wasn't the glory or the credit going to the FBI. It was the plain recklessness he saw demonstrated at the press conference, inflating the shooting even without knowing the situation so that any arrest meant a triumph. Clearly Walker didn't mind the risk of stirring up popular fear and anger if the shooting turned out in the end to be routine. At least the feds are on the alert guarding us all, Cooper thought. That's going to be the message.

He went into Leah's office. She and two junior DDAs were sorting through packets of documents, stapling them, laying them out. She was normally very neat, files in order, floor clear, precise in how books and papers were arranged on her desk. Cooper saw papers haphazardly spread everywhere, and a copy machine that had been dragged into the office churned out more.

She looked up. "We're wrapping up the search warrant affidavit and supporting documents for Booker's home office. Tafoya called and she and Nye are with Booker's chief of staff. So I'm getting together a search warrant for his office too. Might as well get Judge Borden to sign two of them at once." She went on checking papers, stapling.

"I just finished a frank discussion with Agent Walker." The junior DDAs went on working, but he knew they were listening closely. It didn't matter. The whole office and SPD would know soon what was going on. He told Leah in short, bitter bursts.

"I think Walker lost some argument within DOJ. I think Chang won. But he's going to follow orders. He's going to try to beat us to the finish line."

"We've got to do it right, Coop. We can't compromise the investigation just to be there first."

"We're not going to. But the public reaction here and around the country is going to spiral out of control."

"How soon?"

"I bet we've got twenty-four hours, maybe a little more. After that, nobody can tell what's going to happen." He pointed to the carefully stacked copies of the search warrants. "Let's get those out the door, Leah."

SEVEN

"**YOU'RE NOT VERY UPSET,**" Nye said to Manzoni. "You don't even seem surprised your boss is dead."

"I'm devastated. I'm in shock." Manzoni hesitated. "What do I call you? Officer? Sir? Chief?"

"Try Terry."

"Well, I am in shock. June called me. You show up. I've lost a great friend, terrific public servant. It's all going to take a while to sink in."

Nye studied Gil Manzoni. He had a smooth, shiny face and pale blue eyes. He smiled too often. He tapped a silver pen up and down on the pad in front of him. The phones throughout the suite were all ringing and Manzoni's cell continuously peeped "V for Victory." Manzoni ignored them. Rose stood to his left. They had moved him out of his own office to one of the others to get him away from the papers he was diligently annihilating. This office was decorated with intricate maps of Booker's congressional district, webs of lines crisscrossing every city and town. There were other maps of California and the United States and large wall calendars. Manzoni said this was the scheduler's office, where all the planning for the great man's constant movement around the state, the country, and especially his district was laid out in excruciating detail. Manzoni pointed to the maps and a chart alongside them.

"See? Jerry wasn't coming back to California, much less Sacramento, for another week."

"The wife says he told her yesterday he was coming home by the weekend."

"I didn't know."

He went on tapping and a film of sweat shone on his forehead.

"Sure about that?" Rose asked casually. "We'll be looking at your phone records, e-mails."

"Jerry and I talked yesterday and he never said anything. I was with him when he gave his speech, for Christ's sake. Check the TV footage, check a news photo." He flapped the gaudy tie. "You can't miss me. Jerry wasn't going to give the biggest speech of his career without me standing at his elbow."

Nye made a noncommittal face. "Okay. That's easy to check. So that means you flew back here right afterward. You didn't stick around for the talk shows he was going to do today?"

Manzoni leaned back and let a breath out. "The communications staff could handle that. The important thing was to make sure the speech was solid and he delivered it solidly. And he did. That was the strongest speech he ever gave." He looked over at Rose, the odd smile turned on for her. "Jerry wanted me to come back here right away to handle several things."

"Like what? Give me some idea." She waited.

"Line up drinks with several longtime contributors. Help June settle a couple of title matters about the new house, things that needed to be handled."

"You speak to Mrs. Booker about getting together with her today?" Nye asked.

"Yes. I called her and gave her my flight. She picked me up at the airport."

"Some reason Congressman Booker didn't want her picking him up?"

Manzoni shook his head. "No, she had no idea he was coming home. Neither did I."

"What's the stuff you're shredding?" she asked.

"Daily garbage." He paused. "And what do I call you?"

"Detective Tafoya."

"It's standard practice, Detective Tafoya." He almost winked at Nye, who was glad Rose couldn't see it. "Nobody in my profession throws papers into the garbage. You turn everything into confetti. When I was in college, starting out on campaigns, my job was to go Dumpster-diving in the opposition's garbage to see if anything useful got tossed. You'd be surprised."

"I bet," Nye said laconically. "But you know that destroying papers is a no-no from now on, right? This is a homicide investigation."

"I'm a suspect?" He sounded theatrically bewildered. He was someone who frequently spoke for effect. Nye was used to it. "If I'm a suspect, don't I get my rights? I can call a lawyer, can't I, Terry?"

"We're just having an informal conversation, Mr. Manzoni. This is a tough time for you, and Detective Nye and I appreciate your assistance," Rose said.

Nye waited until Manzoni stopped nodding, while he annoyingly kept tapping the pen. Manzoni was posturing enough to alert Nye. *Guy's got a lot he doesn't want to say or let us know. He's figuring how far he can string us.*

That's what happens after you've been a detective as long as me, Nye thought. You read everybody and everybody reads wrong. Even you. Maybe you mostly.

"Why'd he make a big speech about payoffs in Congress? Bet that didn't win him the watercooler popularity contest."

"Jerry said he was fed up." Manzoni rubbed his chin. "He'd seen enough, members going on free trips to the Bahamas, cars and boats, planes all for the asking. Skybox seats for any game you want. The political party label didn't matter. Everybody seemed to be grabbing as much as he could."

"Your guy a Boy Scout?"

"He's a highly decorated veteran. He loves serving his country. He said somebody had to blow the whistle, raise the volume about the winks and nods and freebies so it all didn't go on being only background noise nobody minded." Manzoni frowned. "Jerry told me he was going to blow the roof off the capitol. We had dinner last Friday. He didn't want to waste any time." He stopped. "Christ. When we were having dinner Jerry only had four days left. Christ," he repeated and the tapping pen froze. It was sinking in.

"Mr. Manzoni," Rose said, using the cool, flat voice that wouldn't excite or unnerve whoever was being questioned, "you're Congressman Booker's chief of staff. You make the trains run on time for him?"

"You haven't been around politicians. I do it all." He grinned mirthlessly. "I make sure he's got the right clothes on, he knows who he's talking to every step and when he's got to talk to a guy in a country store out in Isleton or a mortgage banker in San Francisco. I make sure he gets enough sleep, he eats right, he knows his lines every day."

"Doesn't sound like he has to think about too much," Nye said.

"It's a full-time occupation tending a major political figure like Jerry. I've been doing it for him for six years and it's an honor."

Rose nodded. The sense of elevated importance and self-worth radiated from Manzoni in waves. "Then do you know why he lied to you and flew back to Sacramento right after you did?"

"No. I don't."

"You're positive he didn't tell you he was flying in tonight?"

"Yes. I am positive." He bristled.

Nye knew where Rose was leading Manzoni so he picked it up. "Sure, maybe he forgot to tell you, the guy who does it all for him. Maybe he was lying to you," and he waved down Manzoni's protest, "and Booker came back here on a whim."

"I don't know why he came back."

"So what's at 1820 N Street? He meeting someone? He in the market for a downtown apartment?" Nye asked.

"It could be for any reason. Jerry has friends all over California. I guess he could have been apartment hunting too."

Nye nodded. Even he doesn't think I'll go with that one, he thought.

"What about his enemies?" Rose asked, jotting notes, like Nye did, on a small pad. "Any major ones?"

"I need some water." Manzoni got up and they followed him to a small kitchenette off the hallway. More Booker campaign posters adorned the walls. There was a sign-up sheet for a potluck lunch taped to the refrigerator. They waited while he filled a glass from the sink, drank it, and had another. He hung his head over the sink for a second and Nye glanced at Rose, nervous the guy was going to vomit.

When he turned back to them, his face was drawn and slick with sweat. Lousy poker player, I bet, Nye thought. Can't bluff. So what's he not showing?

"Enemies?" Nye prodded.

"Well, Jerry had political enemies. He beat four opponents in primaries the last two elections. It got rough."

"Who did the mudslinging?" Rose asked.

"Jerry always fought to win. He was fair, but we weren't going to lose. He used to say that second-best pilots didn't make it in combat. This was combat."

"What about personal enemies, Mr. Manzoni?" Nye asked.

"I can't think of any. Jerry was one of the most likable guys you'd ever meet. One on one, everybody loved him. You never want to go from the Longworth Building to the House with him. Takes forever." Manzoni's eyes were moist. "Staffers, members, ladies who ran the elevators, garage attendants, they all stopped him and he talked to everybody."

"You get any hate mail recently? Threats?"

"Nothing unusual. A few crazies every week. I turned them over to the FBI. We got five hundred e-mails yesterday and the calls were starting too after the speech. It was about an even split, some thanked him, the rest said he was a lying bastard."

"Maybe somebody really didn't like what he said," Nye offered.

"I've thought about that since June called. I hope to God that's not what happened. I tried to talk Jerry out of making the speech. No gain. Lots of pain. He doesn't have to run for another year. We'll come up with a better issue before then."

Always in the present tense, Nye thought. Life goes on. Except it doesn't. It stopped about ninety minutes ago. For good.

"How about anybody else we should talk to? Any other names?" Nye asked, writing as Manzoni began with Booker's staff employees and some of his prominent local supporters and old friends.

Rose said, "I think I left my pen back in your office, Mr. Manzoni."

Nye went on writing, nodding, and Manzoni was too distracted to acknowledge that she had left. She and Nye had run this one fairly often.

Rose went back into Manzoni's office. She bent down and looked into the shredder. It was a very efficient model and whatever he had been feeding it was indeed nothing more than confetti. That, she knew, was very hard or impossible to put back together. The older or cheaper machines left strips that could be matched, with a lot of painstaking work. But this batch of papers was gone.

The papers Manzoni was about to shred were on top of the machine, where Rose had put them when she took them out of his hand. She flipped through them. It was an odd assortment, real estate brochures extolling homes in the Bay Area and the San Fernando Valley in Southern California, letters from people around the state inquiring about homes for sale. She made notes of the names. The letters were all addressed to Manzoni. Maybe, she thought, Booker was looking for an apartment downtown. Maybe his chief of staff was looking for a new job and a new house.

She came around to his desk. It was a light-wood, slim-lined piece of stylish furniture without drawers so that files or papers had to be put away elsewhere or left on the desk. On top of the pile to the right side of Manzoni's chair was a computer printout boarding pass from the day before in his name, traveling from Dulles Airport to Sacramento Metropolitan Airport. Rose carefully nudged aside the papers underneath so she could see them.

The first few were letters from the Department of Defense, then the secretary of defense, about upcoming votes in the House on various military projects. One letter was an involved explanation of why a senior officer could not appear, as Booker had requested, before the Aerospace Committee. He was going to be in Greenland at the time. She thought that sounded far enough away to be a good excuse.

There were letters inviting Booker to speak at various functions, breakfasts, luncheons, and dinners. The California Black Chamber of Commerce asked him to address a luncheon on the subject of boosting Northern California's economy, and minority employment, by attracting more aerospace industry to the state. Other invitations came from governments in Taiwan, China, and Argentina, asking the congressman to attend trade shows in their countries.

She could hear Nye's droning questions, a few more names, one more address, please. It kept Manzoni occupied.

She turned to the left side of the desk. There was one small gold-framed photo, Manzoni and his wife on a park swing holding their grimacing little dark-haired girl. Nice family, she thought, feeling a pang about her own daughter and the awful, slow-motion decay of her family. Unlike her job, where will and luck and experience paid off, she was appalled to realize that none of them worked at home.

Rose, who had run marathons until recently, didn't give in to personal pain for long. It was something to endure, whatever was happening to Luis and Annorina and her. It would be endured. She had a case right now.

The stack of papers on this side of the desk was much smaller, as if Manzoni had been going through it first. Most of it was reelection related, lists of contributors, lists of supporters in various cities. Possibly important, but it would take a long time to sort out everyone on the lists. Rose lifted her head. Nye said something about Detroit, the signal that Manzoni was on the move.

She put the papers back in order. When she did, a printout slid free. It was sent to Manzoni's e-mail account at the House of Representatives. It was from June Booker. Rose read it:

Saw hr today, G. She refuses. Do u trust her?
I don't. I'm ready for the next step. Call me
when you get in. j

She heard footsteps and Nye's voice. She moved quickly to the office door and almost bumped into Manzoni. He coughed and sniffled. He looked very rocky suddenly.

"Found my pen," she said. "Are you finished?"

Nye nodded. "This's been very helpful. We'll have to talk to you again," he said to Manzoni. "And with your help, we'll arrest whoever's responsible." He passed his card to Manzoni. "We will be in touch."

Manzoni was about to say something when the telephone on his desk, which had been quiet for a few minutes, burred loudly. He glanced at the caller ID. "I have to take this one," he said, wiping his nose with his hand. He didn't seem to have a tissue, so Rose gave him one.

Behind them, Nye and Rose heard Manzoni say, "A senseless tragedy, Governor. No question." Pause. "Christ, Kevin, he'd probably have shot himself if he knew you'd let him lie in state in the capitol." Manzoni raggedly blew his nose.

On the way out to their car, Nye told the uniform cop to go inside and stay with Manzoni until the search warrant showed up. "Don't sit on him, but don't let him get rid of anything."

"Got it," the cop said. He headed into the suite.

"That one's deputy chief material, you watch," Nye said to Rose. "What'd you find?"

"Boarding pass from yesterday, so he did come in when he says."

They got to their car just as the first cold rain fell from the black sky. Nye cursed, sliding into the driver's seat. He started the car and the wipers. "Okay, so he said one thing that wasn't a lie. Anything else?"

"E-mail printout he got in Washington yesterday," Rose said, as they merged into the heavy traffic on University heading downtown. She repeated the message. "I made the call not to ask him about it, Ter."

"Works for me. We still don't know enough to ask decent questions." It was an axiom of police work that information preceded questioning when possible. There were virtues in interviewing witnesses or suspects and committing them to a specific set of facts, but it was often much less productive if the interviewer had little background information. "Okay. So the widow Booker is crabbing to Mr. I Do It All about some unknown woman. What's the beef? Who's the woman?"

"What's the 'next step'?" Rose finished the questions. "June Booker and Manzoni were talking about doing something."

"See, Rosie? Those are decent questions. Did the 'next step' involve Mr. Booker? Maybe Mr. I Do It All did it all. He got here before Booker, lied to us about not knowing, planned it with Mrs. B, and let him have it."

"Why?"

"Oh, come on, Rosie. Don't give it to me," he said in feigned annoyance. "Manzoni's lying about almost everything, I bet. Guy's nothing but angles."

"He shits screws?" she asked. Nye divided most of the world into two classes: those who shit screws and those who did not. Both groups ate nails. Frauds, dissemblers, cheats, the higher ranks in the department, and pretty much everyone they arrested twisted and distorted life until there was little left of the nails.

"Definitely. He knows why Booker was outside 1820 N tonight."

"Let's check out the scene," she said, looking at her watch. "I'll let Cooper know we'll be late to the meeting." She picked up the radio.

Nye chuckled. "I hate making the FBI wait. I hate it."

The rain fell faster and the traffic on the wide streets was black shapes and haloed headlights speeding and vanishing into darkness bordered by rain-blurred colorful business signs.

EIGHT

NYE HAD TO USE SHORT BURSTS of the siren and lights to sluggishly move like a snowplow through the groups of people eddying in the street. Either end of the 1800 block of N Street was closed off by police barricades and at those new boundaries people had massed. It looked, Rose said, as if there were a couple hundred sightseers ringing the block. People held newspapers and umbrellas over their heads. The falling sheets of rain sparkled from the TV lights and the news helicopters' shining lights loudly buzzing back and forth overhead.

By contrast, when Nye parked along the street where the sergeant at the last barricades directed, it was like being inside a strange oasis. Only a few people, most of them cops, and no cars moving. Two bulky Crime Scene vans were angled against the new building at 1820 N and purposeful figures darted back to them in the rain. Large portable floodlights had been set up.

Nye and Rose headed for the temporary shelter of opaque plastic, a large tent that had been erected over the crime scene itself. This was the center of activity.

He shook off the rainwater. "Hey," he called out, "who's in charge?"

"Him," Rose said, pointing at a round man in a yellow official raincoat, gold braid on his uniform hat. "Be nice. It's a lousy day for him too."

They went over to Deputy Chief Miles Layne. He was talking simultaneously on his cell and to a crime scene tech holding a heavy plastic evidence bag of broken glass. "I'm looking right at it, Chief. It's a bottle of Glenlivet. How do I know? It says so." To the tech. "Open the bag. I can smell it. Scotch. Yes. We'd both be rich if we had a buck for every quart over the years. You'd be richer for every quart of tequila you poured down me."

He spotted Nye and Rose. "When this's all over, Chief, we'll quit cold turkey. Heaven help our families."

He ended the call, waved the tech aside. Nye said, "We just talked to Booker's chief of staff and the wife," and he gave Layne a highlighted account.

"It's going to be a long, long night," Layne said. "Come on over here. I've got somebody you should hear."

As they walked across the sidewalk, Rose said, "We've been moving so fast I don't know who's covering this place and the cabdriver."

"Maxwell, Drier, Miller are working on Lorenz and Yellow Cab." Layne had to raise his voice over the helicopters and the rain spattering noisily onto the plastic tent. "Cooper said the FBI's decided we can handle the cabdriver." He spat.

"Yeah, well, they get like that," Nye said, and Rose knew he was aching to say more, but wouldn't to Layne. The deputy chief was an up-through-the-ranks manager and generally liked. It was also common knowledge that Gutierrez had sidelined him recently in favor of advancing others in promotions. They were old friends, but the city council demanded new leadership. This was likely his last major case, and Nye and Rose and everyone in SPD knew it. Including Layne.

"So, here's the place." Layne pointed at the sidewalk in front of the building. Techs were still marking, measuring, and photographing the distances between the two large blood pools, the street, the empty Yellow Cab, examining the cab itself. "Booker got out, Lorenz got out, and they were tidying up the fare when they got hit. Booker had a hundred-dollar bill because Yellow Cab doesn't carry them. He had five more in his wallet. Lorenz had twenties in his hand. There's another forty in the cab."

Rose looked down the sidewalk from the blood pools. "How far away?"

"There's nothing on either body, so at least ten feet."

Guns discharge a fair amount of material in addition to a bullet when they are fired. Some of it is expanding gases from the explosion of the discharge. Some of that discharge, in the form of gunpowder or sooty residue, is left on skin or clothing if the gun is fired close enough.

"Who got it first?" Nye asked.

Layne shook his head. "Who knows? Lorenz got a shot just to the right side of his nose. Booker had time to put his hands up, got a shot in his left arm and then one just below the sternum."

"Any shells?"

"No. We looked all over. Either the shooter picked them up or the gun didn't expend any." Layne, in his raincoat, slightly harried as he snapped instructions to other cops or techs, looked like nothing more than a traffic cop on a rainy night. Maybe Gutierrez's got it right, Nye thought for a moment. It still seemed unfair. Nye also wondered what a push for new faces around the department meant for old hands like him. Rose at least didn't have to worry. She was the department's future.

Rose bent down beside a tech who was tweezering up the last fragments of glass. "The liquor? Booker's?"

"In a brown bag, receipt from a place in Natomas. On the way into town from the airport."

Nye looked at the cab and then walked across the sidewalk, pacing ten feet. He stopped. Six more paces. He was at an alley, also closed off at its far end, with techs and cops in a close line, walking slowly from that end toward him, their flashlights crossing over each other. There were no doors on the 1820 side of the alley. On the opposite side was an overflowing Dumpster and the California Department of Aging. He grunted and went back to Rose and Layne. "Anything from the alley, Chief?"

"Nope. Asphalt and concrete surfaces. No fresh cigarettes or wrappers if anybody was waiting for Booker to show up." Nye imagined the shooter, smoking and grinding out the butts, maybe chewing gum or candy or taking hits from a bottle for courage or stoking the rage to kill. Except that hadn't happened.

"Anybody left in the state building when it happened?" he asked Layne.

"Maybe a Department of General Services cleaning crew. It's a small staff in there and it looks like everyone cleared out at five on the dot."

Rose grinned. "I'm transferring."

"Oh no, you're not." Nye pointed at her. "You ain't getting off the bus before I do." He would hate that. Nye made a wry face at Rose. "Pop quiz, Rosie. What do you think?"

"Maybe a crime of opportunity," she said, glancing at Layne to see how he reacted. "It was a two-eleven." That was the California Penal Code section for robbery. "It doesn't look like the shooter was waiting for Booker."

"I ain't so sure. We can't tell," Nye said, but the unpleasant implication of Rose's last assessment was unavoidable. A killer who knew when and where Booker would be wouldn't have had to stand around. Which, Nye could see Layne and Rose understood, meant that this could be just what the US Attorney said it was, a premeditated killing. A hit.

"No money's gone, far as we can tell," Layne said. "Nothing from either victim, nothing from the cab."

"The shooter got scared away," Rose offered.

"So far we've got nobody who saw the shooting. Couple heard it," Layne said. "Not in the building, not going by on the street. Someone could turn up, you never know. I've got another bunch of you deadweights checking to see if anyone left on foot, got into a car." He looked at his watch. "I've got to give Cooper a call in a couple of minutes, bring him up to speed."

They stepped aside and two techs trundling vacuums and

video cameras went by them. Layne motioned them inside 1820 N.

Rose frowned. "Booker stops to get a bottle and heads over here. He sure sounds like he knew somebody in the building."

The deputy chief nodded. "Let me introduce you."

Leah Fisher anxiously got up from Judge Peggy Roche's dining room table. The judge's husband was in another room watching football on the TV. Leah looked at the grandfather clock against the wall. The judge had been reading and then rereading the two search warrant affidavits.

It's not that hard, Leah wanted to say. Just sign the damn things.

But Judge Roche, a stern, solid woman in her late fifties, wearing an old sweater and faded blue jeans, black-framed glasses pushed down her nose, set her own pace, in her own home and in her courtroom. Leah had experienced the judge's style twice. In an arson case, Judge Roche excluded a burnt mattress that was essential to Leah's case. The detective who wrote the search warrant affidavit, either deliberately or accidentally, misstated where the mattress was found. It was a fatal mistake. She had to dismiss the case. On another occasion, Leah and the defense attorney reached an agreement that there were justifiable reasons for an assault-with-intent-to-kill defendant to get a midterm sentence. Judge Roche had shaken her head. "Well, I think he's an upper term, so, Ms. Fisher, you can take it or leave it."

She took it.

Peggy Roche was the best bet to sign search warrants in a case like this that had to be thrown together, out of necessity, so quickly. She had a reputation for integrity.

Leah heard the Oilers score. She looked at her watch.

"Going somewhere?" Judge Roche asked without raising her eyes.

"I'm sure you can appreciate how fast things are moving, Your Honor."

"And you'd like me to move a little faster too?"

"Not at all."

Leah sat down again. She wore her courtroom expression, neutral and yet determined. "Are there any questions I can answer?" And maybe speed things up a hell of a lot, she almost added.

Judge Roche pushed her glasses back. "If I sign these, Ms. Fisher, I'm going to be famous."

"There's going to be a lot of exposure for everyone on this case, Your Honor."

"But everyone"—Judge Roche carefully stacked the search warrants together—"doesn't have to run for their job like I do. The DA does. You don't. Dennis Cooper doesn't. I have to be careful about how I get attention."

Leah felt her face coloring. "Your Honor, if you're concerned about the affidavits—"

She was interrupted. "So I do have one question," Judge Roche continued as if she hadn't heard Leah. "Is there anything in here that's going to come back and bite me, Ms. Fisher?"

"No, Your Honor. These are rock solid. They'll survive any appeal."

"We both know that every court in this country is going to get a crack at these search warrants and whatever you find as a result." She reached for a plain ballpoint pen on the table, one given out in batches by the Sacramento Trust and Savings Bank. She started signing the multiple copies of the search warrants. "I don't want to look like a dunce. I like what I do too much to get another job."

"I don't want to lose any evidence we collect from these searches," Leah said, standing up, and opening her briefcase.

"Like that arson case we did."

"I learned a great deal from you, Your Honor." *I won't make those mistakes again.*

"I hope so. Dennis always picks the brightest ones." She handed the signed search warrants to Leah, who put them in her briefcase.

Leah didn't know whether the last comment referred to the chief deputy DA's talent spotting or the fact that she and Dennis lived together. If it was the latter, it was an inescapable part of living in a legal community where everyone knew far too much about everyone else.

"Thank you, Your Honor." Leah gratefully headed for the front door. Judge Roche came with her.

"I knew the late lamented Jerry Booker." The judge paused in the doorway. She peered at the rain. "I represented him on a drunk driving case a long time ago." She shook her head in disgust. "What a hero. What a grandstanding fraud. I don't just mean lately. He's the kind of human being who wants congratulations for cleaning up a mess he made."

Leah wasn't particularly interested in Judge Roche's apparently bitter reminiscences. They could swap war stories in the future, when this investigation was over. She thought she'd ask Dennis if he recalled anything about an old case involving Booker.

"Good night, Your Honor," Leah said, hand over her head against the rain.

"We'll find out, Ms. Fisher," and the judge turned back to the football game.

In her car, Leah called Cooper. "Got them signed, Coop. You can start filling up the U-Hauls." She listened, smiled. "I know we're a hell of a team."

"I've lived here since they started selling these units," the elfin elderly woman with faded brown hair said brightly. "I'm one of the pioneers."

Nye and Rose stood beside Deputy Chief Layne in the elegantly avante-garde lobby of 1820 N Street. Steel statues, gnarled wooden furniture, and garish artwork were arranged around them. A uniform cop, raincoat opened, had just started interviewing her for an initial statement. Three other occupants of the building were being interviewed just outside the lobby.

"How long have you lived here?" Rose asked. She smiled. There was a sprightly quality to the elderly woman, just short of being clownish. Even Nye had a small grin.

"One year and one month. I was a senior analyst at the Franchise Tax Board and I invested very wisely. I wanted to have some fun when I retired and believe me, I am having fun." She described the nearby trendy restaurants and bars and the exuberant new nightlife in Sacramento's downtown neighborhoods.

Layne looked at the list of occupants in the building. "You said you know everybody who lives here," and he fumbled for her name.

"Delilah Pennington," she said, and Rose's smiled widened. "We're a pretty close little family, well, some of us. There are a few others, kind of standoffish. Duds, I'd say."

"What about Congressman Booker?" Nye asked. "He standoffish?"

"I still don't know what to think. It's all so sudden. Like a bad movie. It's not supposed to happen on your doorstep."

Both Layne and the uniform cop moved away when his =radio squawked loudly. There was a commotion at the barricade at the far end of the street, and the cops were having trouble keeping the crowd back. Layne handed his building list to Rose.

"The congressman, Mrs. Pennington?" Rose said, taking notes.

"I'm sorry. I get easily distracted now. Believe me, when I worked for FTB, not even 9/11 distracted me."

"Did you see him before tonight, ma'am?" Nye asked in a little exasperation.

"Yes and no. I mean, I never voted for him. I've always voted Peace and Freedom." She looked at each of them expectantly, as if her revelation was astonishing. "And there weren't many of us at FTB," she chortled.

Nye shook his head very slightly for Rose. The old woman had something Layne wanted them to hear, but the path seemed to go through her ramblings. Rose knew what to do. She stood directly in front of Delilah Pennington.

"We need to find out what happened tonight," Rose said. "Please help us by focusing on what happened."

"I said I get distracted." Delilah Pennington's sprightliness faded a little. "I spent so many years doing the same things, it's like being in a candy store now." She squared her tiny shoulders. "What do you want to know?"

"When did you see Congressman Booker before tonight?"

"Well, on television last night. When he gave that speech about corruption and bribery."

Rose noted the sly twinkle. Precise answers to questions, probably how she got through her career handling tax money.

"But if you mean when did I see him in person, that would have been maybe a month ago."

"What was he doing?"

"Coming down the hallway, leaving. It was about six in the morning. I'm up early and I was coming in, and he was going out."

"How many times had you seen him before that?"

"Five or six."

"Does he live here?" Nye asked. "Maybe under a different name?"

"No." She drew the word out. "It depends on what you mean by *live* here. He *stayed* here. With Sandy Drucker on the third floor, unit 316."

Rose ran down the list. "Sandra L. Drucker?"

"Yes. Sandy. She works for the Legislative Counsel over in the capital. She's a lawyer. Very, very nice woman. We talk politics, although she and I don't agree on anything."

Nye asked, "Booker was seeing Ms. Drucker?"

"I don't think many people knew about it. I know very few here even knew." She indicated the lobby. "They were being very quiet about it, she told me. It would hurt him politically. They made a point of not being seen together."

"Did you ever see the two of them together?" Rose asked.

She clasped her little hands. "Once. I was coming out around midnight. I go out late too. It's easy to get very dis- tracted around here, if you want to," and she paused at Rose's frown, "and as I was going out, I saw them just there, in the doorway." She pointed toward the street door. "Kissing. I had to brush by them. It was a real smooch."

"Okay, thank you, Ms. Pennington," Nye said. "I'm going to send that other officer back to take a fuller statement from you."

He and Rose turned toward a bank of elevators. Delilah Pennington called to them, "Are you going to see Sandy?"

"If you wouldn't mind, just wait here, Ms. Pennington," Nye said. "We'll introduce ourselves." He didn't want the old woman alerting Drucker.

The other occupants being interviewed nearby murmured to the cops questioning them.

"She's not here," Delilah Pennington said. Nye's hand stopped at the elevator button. He and Rose went back to the old woman.

"Where is she?" he asked bluntly.

"Well, I stopped by to see her late this afternoon, because I wondered if she'd like to go to dinner at Lucca's or Mikuni's. She said no, she had someone coming, and then we both heard the noise, and then someone yelled in the lobby about a shooting."

"What did she do?" Rose asked sharply.

"We both ran downstairs. Sandy saw what had happened. I was a little frightened, so I stayed inside. I didn't know who had been hurt. I didn't know it was her friend." The old woman sighed very deeply. "Sandy came back and I've never seen anyone so white in my life."

Nye had his radio out. "So where is she, ma'am?"

"I was here in the lobby and I saw her go out with a suitcase. She parks in the garage across the street like a lot of us. I was going to see if I could help, because I knew it was her friend Jerry who'd been shot, but she didn't even look at me, she just kept moving, moving. She said she had to get to the airport. She left just before the police got here."

"What does she look like?" Rose asked briskly.

"Very attractive. About thirtyish, black hair and nice figure. Not so tall."

Nye thought he'd have better luck. "What did you see her go out wearing?"

Delilah Pennington scrunched her little face up. "It was a light blue outfit, no jewelry. Flat brown shoes. She was moving quickly."

Nye relayed that through the radio to Layne and then to Cooper. "Come on, Rosie, we got to go." They hurried out into the rain and strange white lights and the crowd.

"I'll get the airlines to check reservations, see who's booked in the last hour," Rose said.

"We'll see if we got any breaks on this one," Nye said. "Because I sure want to know why this lady's running."

NINE

AS NYE AND ROSE PULLED UP, the rainy sidewalks in front of Terminal A at Sacramento Metropolitan Airport were thronged with people checking luggage, coming in and out of the terminal. A dozen airport security officers, Sacramento County sheriff's deputies, and SPD cops waited for them inside the lobby. The airport manager fell into step as they headed to the Southwest Airline counter.

Nye was in a nasty mood and Rose ran interference for him. "We need you to hold all flights for just thirty minutes, Mr. Metzger."

"And like I said when you called it ahead, I can't hold all flights without FAA approval."

"Then goddammit, get it," Nye snapped. "Christ, I can't even get a straight answer if she's already flown out of here."

The people in the terminal parted for the grim-faced group when it got to the airline counter.

Rose said to the airline supervisor, "What have you got about the person we're looking for?"

The supervisor, tall and middle-aged in a dark sweater with a tiny airline emblem below the left shoulder, started tapping at one of the counter computers while passengers eyed things with curiosity. "We've had a computer hiccup. Our reservation system went down partially and we've only gotten it back it up. I could only get the name before. There. Okay. Now I can give you some answers."

Nye swung to Metzger. "So how come you're not getting that authorization?"

Rose looked up as a group of men and women came up to them. "Please stay back," she started to say.

"FBI," the trim crew-cut man in the lead said. "I'm Agent Belden. We're taking point on this investigation."

Nye stared at him. "Like hell, kid. This is our witness."

"Detective, could you step over here with me for a minute so we can work this out?" Agent Belden said with sharp politeness.

Rose put her hand up. "Hold it, guys. There's more than enough to go around."

Nye stepped toward the FBI agent as the airline supervisor, sounding like a sorrowful quiz show announcer, said, "It looks like a late booking, flight 1456 to Los Angeles in the name of S. Drucker." He tapped again. "That flight left on time about twenty-five minutes ago."

Nye swore. The FBI agent was already on his radio.

"I'll tell Cooper and we'll alert LAX and LAPD when she lands. When's the flight arriving?" Rose demanded. The supervisor was still peering at his computer.

"Correction. The flight went out on time. The passenger didn't. She was a no-show." He looked up. "Sorry for the confusion."

Nye swung away and said to Agent Belden, "Okay, kid. Your call. What's next?"

"I'm just checking now for instructions," the agent said, opening his cell phone.

Nye and Rose walked a few feet away. Rose studied the faces, young, old, smiling, annoyed that swirled by them.

"She's around here, Ter. I don't know what happened, but she's flying out of town."

"Yeah. So let's go find her." He nudged Rose. "We are a damn good team."

Cooper and Leah watched one of the four televisions that had been set up in the makeshift SPD command center on the third floor of the aging granite police department building. Eight FBI agents and SPD detectives sat at the conference table, papers strewn in front of them. Recent video footage of Jerry Booker and the president inspecting the latest sleek-winged jet fighter ran as the young woman announcer said, "The White House had no comment on reports from the Middle East that at least two groups are claiming responsibility for the shooting tonight of Congressman Booker. An unconfirmed report warns of more assassinations. A spokesman for the president said that all national and state agencies are fully involved in the investigation." The announcer shifted. "And in California, the governor has directed that the body of the slain congressman will lie in state in the rotunda of the state capitol starting tomorrow. The governor, a close friend and political ally of Congressman Booker, said . . ."

Cooper turned away.

Leah blew out a slow breath. She held an armload of file folders and she dropped them onto the conference table. "I can feel it, Denny. Like it's actually something you could touch, starting to move out there."

"Remember the Lonsdale police shooting? We were two seconds away from a mob attacking this place." He shook his head. "This feels precisely like that. And it is moving."

He instinctively reached out and squeezed her hand. Sometimes that was all you could do when the mountains began to shake. She held him tightly, then let go.

Walker was on his radio at the head of the table. In addition to the new televisions, an array of communication equipment, desktop computers, and white boards had been set up. Locked steel file cabinets were also placed around the room.

"All right," Cooper said, "let's get started. Agent Walker can catch up when he's finished. Agent Zilaff? Can you hear me?"

From out of the starfish-shaped telephone in the center of conference table Zilaff said, "I can hear you fine."

"How are you coming at the Booker home? Any trouble?"

"It's gotten pretty crowded in the last hour, but I've got agents keeping people away from the home office. We're boxing up the computers, files, some memory sticks, zip files. It's going to take a while to go through all of this material."

Walker brusquely snapped off his radio. "Zilaff, what do you have right now?"

"Couple of things to drill down on. First, the house's new and it looks like it was some kind of swap for their old property. It looks like the swap was a financial loser for the new buyer. Booker and his wife cleared"—there was the sound of papers and fumbling—"about three-quarters of a million on the deal."

"No surprises on that one," Walker said. "What else?"

But Cooper looked quizzically at Leah. She pointed to her files and shook her head. The information might not surprise Walker or the FBI, but Cooper wanted very much to know what it meant. He was going to push Walker hard for the files on Booker.

Zilaff said, "This will take a lot of crosschecking to confirm, but I think Booker had a significant amount of undeclared income in the last eighteen months. Before the house deal was going through, he and his wife bought expensive furniture, three expensive cars, and a boat."

"What kind of boat?"

"A big boat."

Leah said, "What about the furniture? How does that look out of line?"

"I've counted fifteen antique armoires."

"That might be a little excessive," Cooper said. "Anything else, Agent Zilaff?"

"Mrs. Booker is being very cooperative. It's starting to look like a wake here. She's planning to go to the hospital in the next hour."

"We'll have somebody with her," Cooper promised. He noted that Walker was preoccupied about something.

They went through the status of the investigation briskly. Walker's additional agents were due in by midmorning. The seizure of material from Manzoni at Booker's district office was going ahead uneventfully. Manzoni had left, SPD following him home and remaining outside, partly for crowd control but largely, Cooper said, to make certain that Manzoni didn't leave unnoticed. Cooper said they were tracking down the telephone records for the last twenty-four hours for Booker, his wife, and Manzoni.

"What do we know about Lorenz at this point?" Leah asked the four SPD detectives at the table. She wrote the data in green on one of the white boards. They would fill the white boards completely as information came in.

Drier, the most senior, read from a file folder, "Unmarried, twenty-eight. He's been with Yellow Cab for about two years. He's a reliable driver. Never been written up for anything. He's got a couple of regulars who ask for him. Today he clocked in at noon, as usual, no appointments. He dropped off two fares, then circled out to the airport and joined the cab line. Things were slow until about five and then he got Booker, luck of the draw."

Leah said, "So it was just accidental that he and Booker linked up?"

"Absolutely. He was just the next cab."

Drier closed his file. Cooper thought of the million details that went into every crime and how often he had seen that altering merely one or two would have made the crime impossible. Sometimes it was as mundane as waiting an extra second or two at a stop sign or holding a door open for someone. It was the little things that seemed to dictate life or death, and he had begun to wonder, after so many years as a prosecutor, how much luck or fate weighed in the balance of events. He glanced at Leah. He was starting to understand her deep fear that maybe their jobs were pointless. Choices were illusory and only crude mechanics ruled the world.

But he forged ahead anyway. Maybe illusions were the best you could hope for.

Now he said, "I think we can put the Lorenz aspect of the investigation on the back burner, Agent Walker. I think it's a better use of our joint resources to focus on Booker. Particularly since it looks like he had a mistress and she's missing at the moment."

Instead of answering, Walker said to the group at the table, "I want a midnight status meeting, all right? Everybody back here with some answers about who Booker called, who called him, who his wife was talking to. And Zilaff? Start crunching the numbers. I want to know how much money Booker was putting out when this house deal was going on."

Zilaff hung up and the group got up, heading for their offices or cars. Walker faced Cooper and Leah.

"Agent Walker?" Cooper said irritatedly. "It's time to combine efforts on Booker." He pointed. "I'd also like to see the files you promised now."

Leah leaned to him and whispered, "I've got something on Booker, I think."

Cooper nodded almost imperceptibly to her. The FBI's high-handedness was frustrating and dangerous in this case. At best it hurt efficiency on the joint investigation. At worst it meant that there would be squabbling and disagreements and witnesses or evidence could be misread.

Walker straightened his solid blue tie. He had made a decision obviously. "Change of plans on the files, Cooper. They're not available. I'm not convinced the Lorenz angle is insignificant. Your folks need to keep after it."

"Unacceptable," Cooper said. "We both know that Lorenz was probably an opportunistic killing."

Leah studied Walker while Cooper spoke, then she said, "For the sake of argument, suppose the county agreed, what do we get?"

Walker turned to the door. The large wall clock, its white

face yellowed with age, said eight thirty, a reminder of how little time had passed since the killings and how fast events had
moved already.

"You get a trade," he said.

"Meaning exactly what?" Cooper snapped.

"Information for you. Booker's lady for us."

Terry and Rose strode past the food court, its ring of fast food
operations very busy. His stomach growled and the sweet,
spicy smell of fresh cinnamon buns at a nearby stand made his
mouth water.

"We didn't get dinner," Rose said. "Anybody watching?"

He did a quick check. They had split off from most of the
FBI agents and the other law enforcement officers. The airlines
serving Sacramento reported three other possibles using a com-
bination of names ending close to Drucker. He and Rose were
going to Gate 34 to check on one.

"All clear," he said. Four airport security officers were trail-
ing behind them, imperiously examining every face and gate as
they passed.

While Terry kept an eye on them, Rose darted ahead. She
came back a few moments later and handed him a thick, warm
cinnamon bun. "Sorry. It was the only one without a line."

"A stomach like mine, you know what this'll do to it?" But
he bit off a chunk gratefully.

Gate 34 was packed solidly with vacationers, families, a few
businessmen sitting and working on their laptop computers. But
most of the passengers were lined up, starting to board the A row.

This flight went to Ogden, Utah. Rose indicated with her
head that he should start looking through the people at the right
side of the gate. Terry hoped that Drucker, if she was there, was
still in the boarding area. Being confined in the plane made it
easier to keep her in one place, but it could be miserable getting her off it if she decided to be difficult. There was no way of
knowing what was going through her mind now.

The airport security officers had joined them, all of them looking across the people and what they were wearing. Some people stared back, suspicious or even hostile. Most ignored the scrutiny.

Terry moved slowly into the mass of passengers. Several older women, a young woman and her family, he ticked them off, just as he saw Rose doing. None of them were the right age or in the clothing Drucker was reported wearing. He sighed. His fingers were sticky with the bun's icing and he didn't want to get it on his badge or his gun if he had to go for either.

He turned a little to the left, pushing by a very fat black woman who shoved him slightly. The airport's public address announcements echoed loudly and under them, the constant buzzing of many voices and the drone of the same stories from TV monitors about Booker's shooting. He glanced over at one monitor. A knot of people watched it intently.

When he turned back, he spotted Rose moving very purposefully toward the A row that was snaking its way into the aircraft. Then he saw Drucker.

She was five people back from the head of the line as the attendants checked the electronic tickets. She had a large tan bag slung over her shoulder, her ticket in one hand. She looked out the wide windows that ringed the building, out into the rain-swept tarmac and the aircraft lit up just below her, engines revving. So close now, she must be thinking.

Drucker looked back into the boarding area just as Rose and the airport security officers pushed forward.

"Ms. Drucker," Rose said sharply, "we're police officers. Please step out of the line and come to me."

Drucker froze and the people immediately beside her moved away. Terry was almost up to Rose when one of the airport security officers reached to take Drucker's arm.

Terry reacted to the tan bag as it swept out in a wide arc. He ducked slightly, reaching for his gun. Rose ducked too, but the bag hit her flat against the head and she reeled back. Drucker let the bag go and brutally shoved her aside. With athletic grace, Drucker sprinted through the people at Gate 34, who automatically opened a path for her.

Terry ran after her, his gun drawn. Rose was beside him, then ahead of him, and they both shouted at the running woman to stop. But Drucker didn't slow down and picked up speed, heading for the boarding area of the last gate in the terminal. It was empty. Terry shouted again, and Rose was rapidly catching up to Drucker.

Drucker slowed, realizing too late that she had gone the wrong direction and that the terminal ended here. The black wet night gleamed beyond the windows.

Rose closed in as Sandy Drucker dived for the nearest door, burst through it, setting off a jangle of sirens and flashing red lights. His breath husking, Terry dashed down the concrete staircase onto the tarmac, rain spattering him, and tried to catch up. Rose and Drucker ran a twisted course between jet fuel trucks and idling aircraft. With dismay, Terry felt a sharp stitch grip his side, but he ran anyway. He could see that Rose was narrowing the distance between her and Drucker.

Rose shouted again, then threw herself forward. She hit Drucker and they both sprawled awkwardly on the tarmac. Rose had Drucker's arms pulled back swiftly, pinning her, putting handcuffs on her as Terry got up to them.

"You okay?" he hoarsely asked Rose.

"She's killing my arms," Drucker yelled.

"I'm fine, Ter," Rose said and they both pulled Drucker upright. The rain had already matted their hair down as they started back for the terminal. The airport security officers and the FBI agents were bounding down the concrete stairs to meet them.

"What're you running for, lady? You hit a police officer," Terry said with more bemusement than anger. He holstered his gun. His side hurt like hell. He had always loathed chases even when he was younger. Now they just made him feel very old.

"Let go of me," Drucker barked to Rose. She was not out of breath at all, which annoyed Terry. Rose held her tightly by one arm. "I didn't know who you were."

"Well, who the hell did you think we were?" Terry grumped.

Agent Belden, seeming unaware of the drenching rain, reached for Drucker. "We'll take her now, Detective."

"I don't think so," Rose said quietly, firmly, and implacably, continuing to walk, her eyes straight ahead.

"You volunteered to share those files," Cooper said to Walker. "I don't feel like horse-trading for them now."

"Sorry, Cooper. That was a couple of hours ago. I'm under new instructions that I can't disclose ongoing investigative targets."

Leah folded her arms. "Whose instructions?"

"The US Attorney."

"I'll call her," Cooper said, turning to leave. The old police department building invariably discouraged him and he never wanted to spend more time than necessary in it. It was patched, the floors uneven, files and boxes stacked everywhere, and the sour sadness, anger, and fear of thousands upon thousands of people who had moved through it over sixty years were entwined in the very layers of the dingy white-painted walls. At that moment, he barely felt in control of his temper.

"It's final, Cooper," Walker said. He looked at Leah. "But I've got a few things I can give you without violating my instructions." He clearly calculated that she was more pragmatic on the issue than Cooper.

Leah studied him for a moment. "We're listening."

Cooper was angry at the blackmail, but at an impasse. She was right to probe what Walker would reveal.

The special agent said, "I'll give you the name of someone in Los Angeles, someone you can talk to about Booker. You draw your own conclusions. I'll also give you Ralph Payton." He grinned at Leah. "Probably the biggest lobbyist in DC or here, right? He takes in more fees in a month than the three of us combined make in ten years. You're probably about five minutes from coming up with him anyway."

"These childish games are idiotic," Cooper said. "We're on the same side."

"There are a lot of sides to the same side," Walker said. "Deal or not?"

Leah said to Cooper, "I say deal."

He thought for a moment and then reluctantly nodded, shoving a pad across the table to Walker.

"The names and addresses, Agent Walker." Cooper dialed his cell. "They better be worth it. I'm going to hear about this for a long time."

When they got back inside, Terry shook the water off his overcoat, wiping his hand on it. "I got icing on my gun," he complained to Rose. She chuckled, and Sandy Drucker, constantly complaining, cast nervous glances across the terminal corridor. Belden and his agents grimly followed.

"You're way out of shape, too." Rose wondered what Drucker was so wary about.

Before Terry could tell her that he was in great shape, pound for pound at his age, his cell went off. "It's Cooper," he said as he answered.

TEN

"GET OVER IT, TER," Rose said as she drove south on I-5, windshield wipers working frantically to clear the rain. "Move on. Like me."

"Goddammit, I am not going to forget about a bust taken away from us just like that. It's like we're a couple of chumps."

"I was the one she smacked," Rose said. "But I know we got to stay on the main deal. See what Booker's widow says about Drucker. That's got to be a big piece here."

"You want to bet the fibbies come in and take that, too? Goddamn." Terry worked himself up. "I bet they don't even charge Drucker with slugging you."

"I'll grieve it to the union, okay?" She smiled at him. "Don't let it get under your skin."

He slumped down, his overcoat damp, his hands still sticky, and the humiliation of having to turn over Drucker to the FBI—because Cooper said that was the arrangement—freshly smoldering inside him. "Rosie, after so many years and so much crap from so many people for so many reasons, maybe I'm just at my limit. Maybe I'm done, like Layne. He's a short-timer. Maybe I am too."

"You're my inspiration," she said jokingly. "The rest of the detective bureau told me, hey, if Nye can make detective after all those years, go for it."

"I mean it," he repeated stubbornly. "I've been around too long."

"You love to feel sorry for yourself," she said not entirely lightly. "Up there with Luis. He's got the record, moping around the house, can't get a good job, people dumping on him, too much trouble to hold his end of taking care of Annorina."

"Not the same thing. That's home. You expect everybody to try to play you," Terry said, thinking of his own marriage and its frequent stormy interludes. His solution had been to spend more and more time on the job, not a brilliant police officer but one who put in very long hours and tended to all of the details and had an instinct for how people acted and what they felt. The result had been a divorce and two grown kids, living in Arizona and Nevada, whom he had not seen in a year. He was a grandfather by his daughter in Nevada and he had only a picture in July of the baby. He was really starting to feel the weight of many mistakes and missteps.

Rose lapsed into silence, intently watching the road. There was little visibility, even as they swung onto I-80 and the looming skyline of the green glass and concrete federal courthouse, the newer rising steel and stone office monoliths, ghostly lit up in the rain. Their radio burbled a stream of calls and commands. A fair amount dealt with deploying more cops to locations around the city as the news reports focused on the state capital and the governor, Booker's home, and the crime scene itself.

Terry felt guilty. He had discouraged her or made her worry about her family. He sniffed casually, trying to fix it by switching to the investigation. "What made Drucker take off, you think?"

"She's scared about something. She's guilty about something. That lady Pennington puts her in the clear for the shooting, so it's maybe something else."

"Maybe," he said, looking out his window. The older neighborhoods, neon-framed businesses, and blocks of single-story homes rushed by. "What's she scared of?"

"Whoever got Booker," Rose said, checking the directions to the Booker home in Carmichael. Cooper, with barely concealed bitterness, sent them to reinterview June Booker and to locate and bring in Ralph Payton the lobbyist at a restaurant downtown. She and Terry decided to see Mrs. Booker first. Their next assignment was to be on the first flight to Los Angeles the next morning. They had a witness to see in Hancock Park, a present from the FBI, and a big question mark. Cooper's briefing hadn't been extensive, but he said that was all he had to pass along. He'd have more, he hoped, by the midnight sit rep. There was more than enough to keep them very busy, Rose felt strongly, without letting personal animosities or professional problems get in the way. "I'm keeping a really open mind. We don't know enough about Booker to make any call yet. So what's the deuce you had him on?"

"Jeez." Terry thought for a moment, glad they had shifted from the uncomfortable family disquiets he had detoured them onto. "Long time ago now. I was doing patrol around the capital, maybe like twenty years ago." He cleared his throat because Rose had been correct. He was, at that time, an embarrassingly senior patrol officer even as a sergeant, his advancement snail-like and the source of quarrels at home.

As the rain and highway sizzled, he told her about following a late-model green pickup from Capitol onto F Street, and down almost to the freeway on-ramp at Twenty-eighth. It was midafternoon, just before Labor Day and unseasonably hot, maybe close to the century mark. It was a stifling, dull day and the traffic was light and the calls were few and he was bored. He spotted the pickup doing fifty, then sixty down the business and residential streets, well in excess of the speed limit. The driver kept changing lanes too and the pile of chairs, two mattresses, and a basketball standard lashed in the pickup's bed veered dangerously from side to side with each lane change.

"So I figure, what the hell, I got a guy at an oh-eight easy,"

Terry said, referring to the blood alcohol level just below drunk driving at the time. "I got nothing better to do, so I hit it and pulled him over."

Terry remembered sweating even in his summer uniform when he went up to the driver's side of the pickup. The driver was a tall, good-looking airman, in an olive drab flight suit with the name Booker over his right pocket. He had raw dark stitches like little teeth on a nasty wound that ran from his right eyebrow down to his cheek. He was in his early to mid-thirties, smiling, and he was easily a one-oh.

"I'm all set to let him have it, bust him, take him in," Terry said, "and he starts talking to me. He's out of McClellan," meaning the air force base in north Sacramento, "just got back to California from overseas, he's helping a buddy's wife move in, buddy's in the hospital, that's how he got the scar, they were both in a righteous dogfight, he can't tell me where—" and Rose interrupted.

"This was before the Gulf War?"

"Yeah, had to be. Couple years anyway."

"I thought everyone said he got that scar in the Gulf War."

"I guess everybody was wrong." Terry was surprised. "I never thought of that."

Booker went on about how he only had a couple more blocks to go, the buddy's wife lived on the other side of the Rosemount Grill, he'd had a couple of beers with the guys while they loaded up the pickup, Terry recalled. He tapped his knee as details came back.

"Here's the interesting part," Terry said, turning to Rose. "I'm listening to him, I can smell the booze, I can tell he's over the limit, and son of a bitch, I'm buying what he's saying. Yeah, just a couple blocks, yeah, tough break for his buddy, helping the wife, how about a little slack here?"

"You let him skate?" She was incredulous.

"I gave him a reckless and followed him across Twenty-eighth, over Alhambra, down a few blocks. He pulls into a driveway, gets out, and he waves to me. Thinking about it now, I was a jackass, but it all made so much sense while he was talking.

He was good." Terry shook his head. "The best."

"Con men, politicians, pukes, they've all got it. They're sociopaths, Ter." She snorted derisively. "They believe their bullshit. You don't have to."

"What can I say? I bought it. I only did the same once, twice on a flat-out deuce."

"So he goes to Kuwait or wherever, gets some medals, and comes back and runs for Congress couple years later?"

"I think he's been there like ten, fifteen years at least. I never ran into him again."

"You are so lucky," she said. "I could really pimp you on this one."

"Hey, remember our agreement? What we say in the car, stays in the car. You tell me anything, it stays here. And vice versa."

"You're still lucky," she said, jabbing him again. "We're almost there. How do you want to handle Booker's widow?"

There was a long line of people holding umbrellas already even though they were some distance from the Booker mansion. Terry turned to Rose.

"I'll give you a break. You hit her with Drucker and we'll see what pops. You deserve it. You're the one got smacked with the purse."

"Watch out, old man. I can still tell everybody how soft you are."

Terry feigned annoyance. He was happy they were sparring again.

Cooper and Leah walked the three blocks from the Sacramento Police Department back to the District Attorney Building on Ninth and G. He held a large blue umbrella over them both, rain spattering on it. The breeze was cool. They went by the county jail, its concrete and brick bulk starkly floodlit and obscene shouts from inmates at the barred windows wafting down over anybody, like them, who passed by.

Leah had held his arm, then let it go. "What's wrong?"

"I don't like it when I'm not in control," he said simply. "As Agent Walker just demonstrated, we are dancing to his tune."

"He's trying to help, though. Give him that much. You're not mad at me, are you?"

"No," he said, a little insincerely. He was angry with everyone, including himself. "Your judgment was right. We needed to make that deal and keep our hand in the investigation." He thought of Chief Gutierrez, his staff, the whole DA's office perilously close to being sidelined in the most consequential investigation they had ever faced. He knew Leah felt the same litigator's adrenaline rush at the prospect of this investigation, and also the same almost impotent anger that they could not direct it as they knew it should be.

There was also the recognition that they were up fifty stories over the street, without any net, and the fall would be swift, fatal, and irrevocable if they stumbled.

"Denny, Walker may have all of his federal resources." She made them sound trivial. "But Booker and Lorenz were shot in our county. In California's capital."

"I think that makes our position even more ludicrous," he said sourly.

Leah smiled. "He's got the agents. We've got the records."

"You mean at our Department of Justice?"

"Even better. Our case files, DA files, and SPD, the sheriff's department. Booker, his wife, Manzoni, Drucker, Payton, they've all lived here in Sacramento for years, and that means if there's anything, we've got it, not the FBI."

"Then let Agent Walker withhold his files." Cooper smiled a little. "Maybe we'll have something to trade. What did you say a little while ago about Booker?"

They turned the corner and decided to go around to the rear of the squat, late-sixties DA Building. A number of the TV camera crews had remained after the press conference, and neither of them felt like wading through cameras and lights and loud questions. He tilted the umbrella to make it harder to see who they were. The county courthouse, silent and sprawling, stretched out in the rain on their left.

Leah bent to him, close enough that he caught her musky perfume. "Judge Roche was Booker's defense lawyer on some kind of drunk driving case. She wouldn't tell me much but she sounded less than impressed with Booker."

"Okay, let's see what we've got. If we're lucky, it connects to this case. At least it gives us some insights about our victim." He thought about Joyce Gutherie's concern for an old friend gunned down mercilessly. It was a tragedy that would lay bare every vice and only some virtues of the victim and whoever else it touched. There was nothing he could do to change that inevitable outcome.

The tall Chinese elms and pines along G Street and behind the DA Building swayed in the rain-driven breeze as they hurried inside. They took the stairs.

"I'll see what we've got in the law enforcement databases," she said. "I'll check Booker and the rest of them."

"Payton's the wild card. I don't know why Walker's pointed us to him. I know our AG," Cooper said, referring to California's attorney general, "tried to go after him on campaign finance violations, I think. I seem to recall we thought about doing a sting, but our White-Collar Crime Unit shot it down. Do we know why?"

"I can call Aguilar, the supervisor, and find out. I'll gather together anything I can find on Payton."

"One of the biggest lobbyists in the country, and he's a hometown boy," Cooper said when they reached the sixth floor. "Were Payton and Booker in business? What's the connection? Who's this mystery witness in LA Nye and Tafoya are chasing down? What the hell does the FBI have on our victim? We're moving forward blindly," he said angrily. "It's stupid. Dangerous and wasteful."

"I hate losing, Denny. I'll find something," and Leah, in the damp and dank stairwell, kissed him. It was reckless because anyone could have come down the stairs. But Cooper lingered in it with her. There was certainty in the two of them, he knew. Perhaps not much else in their world at the moment, but that at least.

"Change of plan, version 2.0," Rose said, putting away her radio, as they went inside the crowded Booker mansion. "Manzoni got here about ten minutes ago."

"I'll stick to the arrangement. You take the widow. I'll work Manzoni."

Rose nodded. The mansion was very different even after only a few hours. The street and the driveway were solidly filled with cars, cops futilely directing traffic. The large living room overflowed with dark-dressed men and women in clumps, all somber and solemn, a few red-eyed, murmuring and stunned. It reminded her of the pictures she'd seen as a kid of the Kennedy assassinations or King. But even more, it was a familiar scene, the aftermath of every homicide she and Terry had ever worked. It didn't matter whether the great or the unknown fell through unexpected violence, the shock and the upheaval were the same. People just noticed it more when the victim was famous.

She and Terry found June Booker with Manzoni near the large fireplace, her own oil portrait hanging above it. She had changed from the sweatsuit into an elegant and graceful black outfit and a pearl necklace. A small cluster of people, older men and women, surrounded them. One woman held June's hand so tightly the fingers were white.

"Mrs. Booker," Rose said coolly, "it's very important that I talk to you for a few minutes."

Terry stood beside Manzoni. "I need a little bit of your time too. If you don't mind."

It was impossible to misconstrue the frosty glares from the people protectively shielding June Booker. The woman holding her hand let it go and said, "She's going to the hospital to see her husband. Can't this wait?"

Rose felt another surge of frustration. I should know who this lady is, she thought. I've seen that face on TV, in the newspapers. State senator? Board of Supervisors? Somebody important. But all Rose said was, "I'm sorry. Mrs. Booker knows we're only trying to find out what happened as quickly as we can."

The woman started to protest. She was someone who rarely heard firm opposition. June Booker patted her arm. "No, no. I'll take care of it, Cynthia. It's the only way to help Jerry now."

And Manzoni, glancing uneasily at June Booker, said to Terry, "Sure. Let's wrap up whatever it is. Then I'm taking June to the hospital." He made it sound very noble and even courageous.

Terry pointed Manzoni toward the rear of the house. "Come on, we'll find a nice quiet place."

Rose followed June Booker to the kitchen. "I'm afraid your people are still working in my husband's office," she said to Rose. "It's better here."

"This is fine, ma'am."

June Booker spoke to the cook and two women Filipino servants helping her make refreshments for the mourners. They left. Rose watched the servants, who quickly looked away. She wondered if they all had relatives near Cebu City who knew each other, her parents and theirs. The reality of murder was that it wildly jumbled lives, created new combinations and linkages between people who might never otherwise have encountered each other. It still amazed her.

"Mrs. Booker," Rose began, "do you know a woman named Sandra Drucker?"

"Unfortunately, I do."

"Who is she?"

"Ms. Drucker," June Booker said, leaned back against a stainless steel counter, "is a prostitute. Jerry has been seeing her for two years."

Rose caught the bedrock hatred under the calmly spoken words. June Booker's face was a mask.

"Have you ever met Sandra Drucker?"

"No, I have not. I do not intend to."

"Mrs. Booker, we have some indication that you met with Ms. Drucker yesterday."

"Well then, perhaps I did. I've been trying to pretend she doesn't exist, that Jerry hadn't done something so callous to me and his children. I suppose I simply blocked it out of my mind."

"What did you go to see her about?"

"Detective Tafoya, how confidential is whatever I tell you? I'm very interested . . . " She paused and for an instant, Rose thought she heard a catch in June Booker's voice. " . . . in preserving the reputation of my husband now. It's partly selfish. I am thinking of myself and our children. I'm also thinking of the many good things he did, his service record in the Gulf War, the legislation he worked so hard on to make people's lives better in this country. I don't want to see all of that, his life and mine, desecrated by a common whore."

"I can only say that we'll try to keep information unconnected to the investigation confidential. I can't promise anything. But the more you tell me, the more we're going to be able to do."

"I suppose I don't have a lot of choice. But I'm giving you and the police and the FBI fair warning. If there are leaks, I'm going to use every powerful friend Jerry had"—she gave a wintry smile—"and extract a lot of pain from whoever's responsible."

"The police department plays it straight, Mrs. Booker. Why did you go to see Sandra Drucker?"

"She was blackmailing Jerry about their relationship. It would have been devastating to him politically if it was public and she knew it. I went to see her to end the blackmail."

"How long had this blackmail been going on?"

"I believe it started shortly after he first met her. She was interested in Jerry purely for the money."

"How did you plan to stop the blackmail?"

June Booker paced to the elaborate infrared range. "I offered her a lot of money. You might think Jerry and I are rich, but we're not. I offered her everything I could scrape together."

"Did she take the money?" Rose recalled the printout in Manzoni's office. She waited to see what June Booker would say.

"No. She turned me down. I suppose it wasn't enough. I think she was going to go on blackmailing Jerry, getting every cent for as long as she could."

"Did you talk to Mr. Manzoni about Sandra Drucker?"

"Gil was aware of the situation."

Rose had been jotting notes. She paused, appearing to formulate a question, but she had had it in mind from the outset. "Well, if Ms. Drucker rejected your offer, did you and Mr. Manzoni have another option you were looking at?"

June Booker stopped pacing.

"Sure I knew he was seeing her." Gil Manzoni sat on the edge of the bed in a guest room. "Jerry told me. I mean, I would've found out. I know where he is every minute."

"I'm guessing your boss seeing a woman while he's married was a problem."

"A huge one, even today. Would've cut a giant slice out of Jerry's base up north."

Terry nodded. He sat at a dainty vanity table, uncomfortably trying to find some place to prop his elbow while he wrote. "You tell Mrs. Booker?"

Manzoni snorted. "Not for a while. I knew June would go ballistic and I wanted to see if I could get Jerry to call it off."

"And he didn't?"

"Nope. He said he deserved a little peace and happiness and he was going to get it."

"So how did Mrs. Booker take the news?"

"She went ballistic. Jerry moved out for a couple of days, and then June realized that might start questions, so she let him come back. She's been a tad cool to me too because I didn't tell her about Jerry and Sandy right away."

Terry noted the first names, the easy familiarity. "You know Drucker?"

"Not until she and Jerry got together. She was over at Leg. Counsel, but she wasn't into party politics, all our little games, you know." He chuckled but Terry did not. "Sandy's pretty much what you see, smart, centered, a little lonely, I guess. She and Jerry worked out."

Terry tried a shot. "So you and Mrs. Booker, you're talking

the last couple of days. She's all bothered about Drucker, wants it to end. She's going to see Drucker. Is that right?"

"If she couldn't get Jerry to drop Sandy, June thought she'd try to get Sandy to drop Jerry."

Terry gave up trying to sit naturally at the vanity table. He stood. "What did you both come up with?"

"Threats pretty much." He hunched forward. "Get her fired. Make sure she couldn't work in state government again. Make it hard for her to get work as a lawyer anywhere."

"What if she didn't go for that?"

"Well, I told June we could flip it around. Offer her a better job, maybe chief counsel at some agency, maybe even work for the governor in the horseshoe," he said, referring to the inner ring of offices in the state capital that surrounded the governor's office. "Buy her off, I guess you'd say."

"You were bribing her." Terry made it sound mundane.

"A lot of business, perfectly legal, gets done around here like that. It's more like an understanding between people."

"Drucker like the idea of a bigger paycheck or did you scare her?"

"Neither. June sent me a note after they met yesterday. Sandy turned her down."

Terry heard sirens rising and falling, the background sound of his life. Someone on the hunt. A disturbance in the imagined orderliness of life needed to be fixed. Even the simple ones, he had discovered, were never simple. Like Manzoni and the infuriated widow and their problem named Sandra Drucker. Or the dead congressman who wouldn't forget about her. Terry tried to mix the image of that wounded, happy, very persuasive younger airman and the sad last chapter he was learning about now.

"Sounds like your boss knew he didn't have much of a political career left. So he makes this speech and burns a lot of bridges."

Manzoni looked up. "Jerry was going to run again. He would've told me if he was cashing out."

But Terry didn't think there was rock-solid assurance in Manzoni's declaration. "What was the next step for you and

Mrs. Booker?"

"We hadn't discussed it."

"Well, we got those phone records. You and Mrs. Booker. The congressman and you. The congressman and his wife. Lots of chatter in the last twenty-four hours. I think we can kind of"—he made little gestures in the air—"bring it together, Manzoni. You and the wife know Booker's coming to Sacramento. You know where he's going."

Manzoni sprang off the bed, face working in fear and anger. "I told you Jerry was a friend and he was my work twenty-four-seven, okay? I lose him, I lose it all. I've lost it all."

"I bet there are other guys who want to be in Congress."

Manzoni swore and for a moment, Terry thought he was going to lash out. The prospect of punching someone out was not entirely unpleasant after the incident at the airport or Cooper's lousy deal with the FBI. But Manzoni shakily snapped, "I don't what know what happened to Jerry tonight. I didn't have anything to do with it."

"What about Mrs. Booker?"

"June didn't hate Jerry enough to hurt him."

"So, what's your hunch now?"

"I think Jerry was killed for what he said. For the honorable man he was."

Or that's the story you're going to lay out every chance you get, Terry thought.

"Are you done?" Manzoni asked angrily. "I've got to take June to the hospital now. Then there's a lot to do for tomorrow, Jerry lying-in-state. I can't believe any of this nightmare is happening."

Terry opened the bedroom door. The subdued voices floated in. "We still got a lot to go over later," he said. He tried another shot. "I'm seeing Ralph Payton tonight. You know him?"

"Of course. I've been trying to get hold of him ever since this happened, but I can't raise him. June's concerned that he's not here. He and Jerry go back. They're old pals."

"Like how?"

"Vacations, the families together. Holidays together. Ralph owned this house, sold it to Jerry and June." Manzoni pointed around them. "He bought their old place."

Terry kept walking, pretending he hadn't heard anything of interest. But something that Manzoni said fitted with what he'd been seeing and hearing all night. Real estate, he thought. You always keep turning up real estate, at Manzoni's office, Cooper's witness in LA tomorrow, and now this house. Zilaff's back there happily digging around in the home office, an FBI agent specializing in white-collar crime, just out of Seattle. White-collar crime and real estate. There's a connection to Booker.

Terry was mad again. Maybe the dead hero might not be a hero, but the FBI had a whole lot of pieces they weren't putting on the board so you couldn't be sure. He and Rose, Cooper, they were all flailing at shadows because the feds were holding back.

You can make a hell of a lot of mistakes crashing around when someone's got information and won't give it up, Terry thought. And a lot of people, including me and Rose, can get hurt.

And the whole country's watching.

ELEVEN

COOPER AND WALKER STOOD off to one side of the interview room on the second floor of the Sacramento County Jail. They spoke in low voices while Sandra Drucker was brought in and seated in a gray metal chair at the gray metal table in the center of the room. It was an intentionally bare and windowless room, without a clock or any decoration. The two county sheriff's deputies waited. She stared down at the table, hands clasped tightly, and then she sat back and rubbed her eyes slowly.

"All right," Cooper said to Walker evenly, "you ask the questions. But this is part and parcel of complicating the investigation."

Walker glanced over at Sandy Drucker. "I'm helping you as much as I can," he said sharply, quietly. "Look, you know what the USA," meaning their United States Attorney, "is doing back in Washington?"

"Consultations with the White House are what I heard at the press conference."

"She's going back to personally make sure no one, the president or anybody close to him, gets out in front holding Booker up as a martyr."

"Agent Walker"—Cooper was coldly furious— "this is the problem. Why the hell don't you tell me what you know about Booker?"

"Because I don't know you, Cooper," he said bluntly and turned to Sandy Drucker. She was attractive; nervous but trying to hide it. Her mouth trembled involuntarily. She had cleaned up from the chase at the airport, wavy black hair brushed, light blue blouse straightened.

Cooper sat down at the table. Walker sat down and waited. "Would you like water, coffee?" he asked her.

"I would like to know what's going on," Sandy Drucker said to him. Cooper admired her self-control. She was obviously frightened, shocked at being brought in by the police, and yet she was doing a fairly good job of maintaining her composure. Leah had run her through the various automated law enforcement databases, and except for her fingerprinting when she was admitted to the State Bar, Sandra Drucker had no other record. "Am I under arrest?"

"We're reviewing the information, Ms. Drucker," Walker said. He had convinced Cooper to wait on any decision for use as a possible bargaining point with Drucker. "I'd like to ask you some questions about Congressman Booker and his visit to see you this evening."

"Am I being detained?"

Cooper was impressed by her directness. Most people, unfamiliar with arrest or being rudely dumped into the law enforcement system, were either too blustery or too startled to be coherent. Most lawyers who got arrested did no better. But this woman was taking charge of the situation. That was rare.

Walker studied her. "No, you aren't. But I thought you'd be anxious to help us find out why the congressman was killed."

"You have no idea how fucking anxious I am to find out," she exploded, abruptly standing up. The two deputies tensed, but Cooper waved them back. "Someone I cared about very,

very deeply was killed almost in front of me. *I'm* attacked by the
police at the airport—"

Cooper interrupted calmly. "Ms. Drucker, you tried to hide
your flight, didn't you?"

"I haven't done one fucking thing wrong," she yelled. The
self-control dissolved in a surge of fear, anger, and grief. "If you
want to find out what happened to Jerry, ask Ralph Payton," she
said furiously, heading for the door. "I'm going to see if I can't
sue every damn one of you." Walker stood, as if to block her,
then let her by. He was plainly surprised and angered by her
outburst. Sandy Drucker hesitated for a moment, looking back
at Cooper, and then she marched through the door.

"I think that went well, Agent Walker," Cooper couldn't
resist saying slowly. He was intrigued that both the FBI and
Booker's mistress wanted him to talk to Payton.

"You didn't have to come all the way downtown," Leah said to
Justin Aguilar, supervisor of the district attorney's White-Collar
Crime Bureau.

Aguilar was a small, older man with thick glasses and large
eyes. "It's no trouble. It's exciting here tonight."

Leah showed him the California Department of Justice printout on Ralph Payton. It showed two arrests ten years earlier for
disturbing the peace and small fines. "What about Payton?" she
asked. "I thought we were thinking of rattling his cage at least."

"I'd still like to," Aguilar said with a sigh. "I've been getting tips and whispers about him for three years. He's got huge
clients here and Seattle, aerospace and construction, Indian
tribes with a lot of loose cash. He's also got a PDA full of legislators he knows, and everyone reports every dime they spend on
dinners, fishing trips to the Bahamas, and fact-finding missions
to Hawaii."

"Why haven't we put together a sting?" she asked with
curiosity. Leah thought Aguilar had described the ideal target of an
undercover operation, one in which an illegal transaction, money

or contraband or gifts, could be recorded on video and audio.

Aguilar polished his glasses. "Payton's doing deals. I know it. But I can't get anyone to take the next step, come forward and tell me what he's doing, let us wire him and put a camera on a payoff. No sting without a snitch. Payton's been really lucky or he's really careful who he buys."

"Did you hear anything about Payton and Booker?" she asked. "I mean, why was a war hero member of Congress anywhere near a guy like Payton?"

"Money. Money. What else? We've been looking locally at Payton, not at federal officials." He grinned boyishly at her. "I don't recall what Payton did for Booker, but I can check what we have. It's probably same old, same old. Vacation slash legislative trip to a rough place like the Big Island, maybe a speech at the resort to the executives from one of the aerospace outfits. All paid for by the company Payton represents and all reported."

"Everything's reported? I can't believe that."

"Anything you can see, any gift, trip, expense, that's reported. It's the other stuff, cash or drugs, whatever, that's what doesn't show on a Fair Political Practices gift form or a federal report. That's what you need a snitch for."

"Do you think the FBI had a snitch on Payton and Booker?"

Aguilar shrugged. "They could have snitches on him or you or me. Who knows?"

Leah thanked him and thoughtfully punched up Booker in the California DOJ database. An informant working for the FBI on the investigation of a possibly corrupt congressman would explain why Walker wouldn't expose his files.

She watched as Booker's record unscrolled on her computer screen.

An informant might also have a reason to kill Booker.

Terry held his hand out in the breezy night. "Hey. It stopped raining."

Rose muttered something. She had been distracted as they

drove downtown from the Booker mansion, passing the small, compact Chinatown and its grocery stores with exotic produce and large restaurants with neon piping watched over by a heroic statue of Sun Yat Sen, going farther along J Street, a disordered mixture of new office buildings, a barber college, and empty storefronts. They stopped and got out in front of Caspari's, a brick-fronted restaurant oozing light and old piano standards. A young valet jumped for Terry's keys.

"I don't think so, kid. Police. Nice try."

The valet frowned and sat down again.

Rose walked ahead to the door. "You know what's getting to me?" she said, focusing on him after a nearly silent trip. "It's all like an anthill that got kicked. Ants running everywhere, their whole world all messed up. Everything out in the open, no way to hide it."

"That is what's bothering you about this case?" Terry asked in amazement. In their year together as partners, he had never heard Rose express being troubled about more than the logistics of an investigation. It made him uneasy now.

She looked at him. She had her hand on the door. "I keep wondering what would happen if my life, my family got kicked over like that. What would people say about me or my family?"

Terry growled, "Are you kidding? I had a partner whose house got hit, basic daytime smash-and-grab burg. He calls it in, he's all worked up, the wife's all worked up because their stuff has been stolen. So when the techs get out there, all set to do some fingerprinting, take pictures, they can't get through the front door because"—Terry's face contorted comically—"it was wall-to-wall garbage and junk, and you don't want to know what. This guy and his wife lived like pigs and it so was goddamn filthy and messy, the techs couldn't figure out what had been stolen." Terry reached past her to get the door. "They couldn't even decide if they should let the poor bastard who stole the garbage know he might get that flesh-eating bacteria thing going." He pulled the door open and a rush of warm, garlic-and-perfume scented air hit them. "You don't have a pigsty at home, right?"

"You know I don't."

"Then quit worrying about what people are going to see or think. Christ, Rosie, nothing's happened so how the hell does anybody know anyway?"

"Never mind. It's nothing," she said. "Let's find this mope." She forced herself ahead of him into the restaurant. Terry knew she wasn't concerned about a less-than-immaculate house being revealed to the world. For Rose, the shame and disgrace was having a husband who was unabashedly a burden. It was the fear that her colleagues would know about Luis and her struggle to make sure Annorina was brought up well.

Once more, Terry felt the sickening helplessness of understanding what deeply troubled Rose and being unable to do much for her.

Rose walked past the tall older man in a white shirt and a black suit with a port wine stain on the right side of his face who was checking dinner reservations. The mirrored and curved bar, behind which ranks of expensive liquor bottles rose nearly to the ceiling, beckoned invitingly.

"Is Ralph Payton here tonight?" Rose asked him crisply. "We're meeting him."

"The name?" the man asked daintily, grease pen poised over the plastic table layout in front of him.

"Sacramento police," Terry said, eyeing the frantically busy bar and the tantalizing display of liquor. He felt like a man on the hottest summer day coming on a cool blue pool, thinking how magnificent it would be to dive in. And then you, he said to himself, would never come up. He saw Rose's disapproving glance. "I'm only looking," he said honestly. Those days were over, he was certain.

"I think," the port-wine-stained host said, "you'll find Mr. Payton downstairs. With the others."

"Others?" Rose asked.

"Associates," he said.

Terry grunted and they turned down a hallway, at the end of which was the noisy kitchen, and followed a sign down a short stairway. At the bottom was a large, low-ceilinged banquet room, faintly smelling of the river damp. California's capital was built up from its early flood-prone history, but the downtown still sat atop the mud of the Sacramento River.

There were, Terry and Rose noted, about twenty men and women, boisterously drinking and singing. They seemed to have been at it for several hours, judging by the empty bottles, broken dishes, and overturned chairs. A CD played late-eighties rock over the laughter and shouts.

Rose waded through the partygoers. She didn't see anybody matching Payton's description.

"Excuse me," she said to a loudly hollering tall thin man, "is Ralph Payton here?"

"Who the hell are you?" he snarled suddenly.

"We're the police," Terry said. "So you can go on with the party, just tell us if Payton's around here some place."

The man backed down instantly. He sniffled and his eyes watered. The others went on rowdily around them. "Ralph cut out about twenty minutes ago. He's fucking in a lousy mood. Me too. All of us." He drunkenly swept his arm around the room. "Fucking bastards killed Jerry."

"You know where Payton went?" Rose asked.

The man abruptly yelled, "Shut the fuck up, you assholes! Anybody know where Ralph went? The cops want him!"

A woman at the edge of the room said, "I think he's at the capitol. He's going to wait for Jerry."

The room was very quiet. All eyes were on Rose and Terry and they both sensed the barely stifled rage stoked by drinking. "How come you're looking for Ralph?" the thin man asked belligerently. "How the fuck come you aren't going after the bastards who killed Jerry?"

"And who did that?" Terry asked mildly. He knew from personal and professional experience that it was unwise to startle or irritate a roomful of angry drunks.

"Fucking terrorists! We all know that! Time to kill every fucking one of them!" someone in the middle of the people yelled. They nodded, waiting for Terry or Rose to dispute the truth.

"Yeah, we're working on it," he said. "Everybody stay here, have a couple for your pal, keep things quiet, and that'll be great."

He and Rose turned for the stairs.

"You don't get the fucking terrorists, *we will.* Jerry had a *lot* of friends," the thin man sniffled loudly in an angry challenge.

Rose didn't stop and neither did Terry. They were both surprised when, instead of more rough threats from downstairs, a ragged, off-tune maudlin chorus of "Auld Lang Syne" floated after them, topped by a wailing female voice.

Cooper and Walker followed the pathologist across the basement morgue at Sutter General. The room was cool, mint-scented, white-tiled, and steel-fixtured.

They stopped at a steel, grooved table on which Congressman Gerald Booker lay. On an identical table nearby lay Jaime Lorenz.

"We videotaped both autopsies," the droopy-eyed pathologist said, nodding to Walker, "as you requested and I'll get you the DVDs before you leave."

"What did you find?" Cooper asked, his mouth twitching slightly. He had attended few autopsies throughout his years as head of Major Crimes. It was not, he had often told himself, because of squeamishness but more because he saw little value in the unpleasant activity from his point of view. He had reports. He had pictures. He had physical evidence. But once again, in a morgue looking at the wounded, lifeless, resewn bodies, he had to admit it was the unblinking, undeniable, unchangeable stark presentation of inevitable personal annihilation that disturbed him. He hadn't ever been able to find anything he could hang on to that leavened what lay in front of him now. Maybe work and the daily diligence of pursuing order and explanations out of death and violence were all there was for him. It was not, at that or any moment, reassuring.

Walker, by contrast, appeared totally untroubled. He could have been looking at a dead cow or an engine block. He drummed his fingers along the edge of the autopsy table.

The pathologist handed two plastic evidence bags, tagged with his name and the time the bags were sealed, to Walker. Cooper didn't object.

"Both victims were killed by .38 slugs. The Lorenz bullets are less intact than the ones we got out of Congressman Booker, but I think you've got enough to check."

"You mind doing the honors?" Walker gave the bags to Cooper.

"I'll have the crime lab run them through the system." He meant automated processes that compared the rifling and uniquely identifying marks of a fired bullet to millions of records of other fired bullets. The results might locate matches for other bullets and the guns that fired them. The FBI used California's modern state crime lab on Broadway to access the ballistics databases.

"Doctor," Cooper said, anxious to leave, "is there anything you're going to put in your report that distinguishes these shootings? Anything we can use?"

The pathologist shook his head. They walked away from the tables. Hospital attendants in white came forward and started to move Booker's body into a burnished brown heavy-gauge steel casket. "We've been getting pestered every fifteen minutes from the governor's office," the pathologist explained. "They want to know when we'll be finished so the congressman can get over to a funeral home, get embalmed, and then displayed in the state capitol."

"What about the shootings?" Cooper asked again, as the pathologist used a key card to open the morgue doors.

"There's nothing unusual," he said. "If I didn't know who Congressman Booker was, I'd say this was a shooting like every other one you and I see, Dennis."

The three men went over when the pathologist's official report would be ready, by early morning, and he gave Walker and Cooper each a DVD of the two autopsies. Cooper turned the bullets over to an agent from the attorney general. The California attorney general operated the state crime lab, and everyone, Cooper knew, wanted to be very visibly seen as part of the fast-moving investigation.

He and Walker waited for an elevator to take them to the first floor.

"The governor isn't getting the benefit of Ms. Chang's warning like the president, is he?" Cooper asked Walker.

"I work for the president. The governor of California is on his own if he wants to honor Booker."

The elevator opened. They got in. "Nye and Tafoya are having a little trouble finding Payton," Cooper said. "He was at some kind of impromptu wake and he's moved on. They're looking for him."

"Payton's around. He won't go any place too far until he figures out what's happening."

Cooper suppressed annoyance again. Walker had gone right to the edge of admitting what Leah suspected now, that an investigation of Booker and Payton involving an informant had been going on. Cooper didn't tell Walker that Leah was tracking down Booker's past through their county records at that moment.

"Two hours to the next situation report," Cooper said. "I'm afraid we're not going to have much to show. Still no witness to the shootings, and the people closest to Booker can account for themselves at the time of the shootings. I hope the bullets turn up in the system. At least with another match we'll have some lead."

Walker said, "There's going to be at least one big change by the time of the meeting."

He sounded, Cooper thought, distinctly frustrated, as if having his boss, the US Attorney, back in Washington soon advising the White House wasn't a great advantage for him too. "What's happening?"

Walker put his hands in his pockets dejectedly. "Homeland Security is going to bump up the national threat level to red in forty minutes."

Cooper knew what that meant. Regardless of what the FBI and the US Attorney said privately about Booker being under suspicion for some illegal conduct, his murder was being treated as a national security threat. The vast nationwide law enforcement and military machinery would become very public. People's unease and paranoia would ratchet up quickly.

"We really don't have much time," Cooper said.

"No, Mr. Cooper, we do not."

TWELVE

IT DIDN'T TAKE LONG for Nye and Rose to find Ralph Payton when they got to the state capitol. "I really want to know why the FBI's handing us this guy," Rose said. They were both anxious to talk to Payton. A phalanx of uniformed Sacramento Sheriff's deputies, state police, and California Highway Patrol officers carrying assault rifles tightly ringed the grounds of the large white wedding cake building. It was eerily dark. The normal floodlights that made it gleam at night, opulent and only a little less imposing than the nation's capitol, had been shut off for security reasons. Police cars and barricades filled and closed the streets surrounding the capitol.

A CHP officer Nye knew met them on the east-side steps of the building.

"Hey, Estrada," Nye said, "what's going on?"

The CHP officer had Payton by the arm. "We're holding the fort. National Guard's supposed to take over in couple of hours." He gently pushed the man toward Rose. "This guy tried to get past the perimeter. Said he wanted to sit on one of the benches under the trees and get loaded."

Payton smiled crookedly at Rose. "I'm sentimental."

"Okay, thanks, Estrada. We'll take him. Hey." He looked at the milling collection of uniforms and guns, the nervous voices and radios crackling. "You take care."

Rose and Terry walked with Payton between them, passing through the ring of cops. Across the street, the Library and Courts Building, an ornate granite temple built at the time of the First World War for the Supreme Court, suddenly lost its nighttime illumination, as did the state Treasurer's Building opposite it. The center of California's government was going dark after the storm in the breezy, cool night.

"Mr. Payton?" Rose asked. "Have you been drinking?"

"Very happily," he said with a slight Southern drawl. "I had a nice single malt all set to go while I waited for my old friend Jerry Booker to arrive in style. It was confiscated."

Ralph Payton was in his late forties, lanky and balding, with red-flecked cheeks from blood pressure. He was tall and soft and he had on a stiffly starched white shirt, a green-and-gold-striped tie, loosened. His expensive gray suit was finely tailored.

"We'd like to ask you about Congressman Booker," Rose said. "Do you mind coming to the police department now?"

"Are we just talking here? Am I a suspect or something?" He slurred his words and he wobbled a little on his feet.

"Just talking, trying to find out as much as we can," Nye said. "How about it?"

"Well, if we're talking and I'm going to be denied welcoming my old friend on his final journey"—he licked his lips—"come on over to the Sutter Club." He pointed across the street. "And we can act like normal people even when it's not really normal at all."

Rose looked to Terry. "Yeah, sure. We can do that."

He and Rose both knew that if a witness or possible suspect felt relaxed and comfortable, he might answer questions more freely. At that point, they couldn't hold Payton anyway.

Payton, with a few stumbles, led the way. Rose silently mouthed her guess to Terry that Payton's blood alcohol was a one-one. He figured even a one-two. The Sutter Club was in a Spanish colonial building and it had been the chosen refuge of the business and political elite of Sacramento for a very long time. Payton brought them through the red-tiled lobby adorned with group pictures going back decades featuring governors, legislators, and a few United States senators who were members, into an expansive dark-wood-beamed room with musty books and a sooty fireplace with an obscure escutcheon over it. "This is perfect. It's the library. Nobody ever comes in here."

He sank into an old but very accommodating leather chair and motioned for Rose and Nye to take the other chairs. A white-jacketed Hispanic waiter swiftly appeared. "Good evening, Mr. Payton," he said as if it was a night like any other. "It's very sad about Mr. Booker."

"Yes, Paul, it is very sad," Payton said. "I'm having a double single malt. Does that make any sense, Paul? My guests." He waved at Rose and Terry.

"Nothing, thanks," Nye said, pleased that for the second time that night true temptation had been put in his path and Rose had seen him reject it.

Nye had his pad out on his knee. "How long have you known Congressman Booker?"

Payton sat back, slack and glassy-eyed. "Ten years. Our families are close, we take vacations together. We went to Peru last year." He momentarily got lost in a reverie.

"You bought the congressman's old house," Rose said. "Kind of overpaid for it."

"The real estate market around here was very hot for a little while and then it popped overnight." He made a sound. "Bad timing for me, but it helped June and Jerry so it wasn't a loss at all for me."

"Could look like you gave him about three-quarters of a million dollars."

"Nobody's got that kind of money to give away." Payton crossed his long legs, and his right foot bounced up and down. "I certainly don't. I don't have any reason to anyway."

There were a few voices coming out of the grill on the other side of the hall as members drifted in or left. Rose glanced around. Payton smiled wanly. "We admitted women about twenty years ago. It was a very correct decision."

Rose looked at him. "What was your business relationship with the congressman?"

"Well, first we're friends. That's on top of anything else. I've got a number of clients here in California and in Washington State, aerospace companies," and he casually rattled off major names, "and Jerry's the chair of the House Aerospace Committee. I try to keep him, as an old, old friend, aware of what the industry's doing, what its key players are thinking. Good for California. Good for the country."

Good for you and old Jerry, Nye thought.

The waiter silently appeared and left Payton his drink. He raised it and sipped and licked his lips a little.

"So that's the vacations and the trips you mentioned," Nye said, "to keep him up to date while your wives and kids sightsee?"

"Listen, Detectives." Payton sipped again. "I'm a registered lobbyist here and in Washington, D.C. Every dime I spend or take in is fully and publicly reported."

His drawl was still soft and sibilant, but Nye detected a hard undertone.

"Every dime that Jerry got from a nonprofit entity for a business trip or from one of my clients in his official capacity, well, he reported that and that's all public too. Check with his chief of staff, Gil Manzoni. He's got all the paperwork."

"He was shredding a lot of paper this evening," Rose said.

"Nothing he shouldn't, I'm sure."

Nye liked Payton's nonchalant smoothness. He didn't trust it at all. But he'd come to appreciate people who could carry it off. It was depressing to interview suspects and witnesses whose patter was transparently phony. Stupid, too. Payton was like watching a superb skier or ballplayer.

"You know how much all of this travel and keeping up to date brought in, Mr. Payton?" Rose asked. "A guess?"

"I billed about ten million dollars last year. Keeping Jerry and aerospace leaders in touch." He sipped again, licked his lips again, and drawled, "Probably a million or so."

"A good chunk of your income," Nye said, waiting for Payton to say more.

"My clients need the service I provide," he said. "Jerry was able to bring about three thousand jobs to California in the last two years, attracting aerospace companies here. Big boost to our economy." He raised his glass. "And a lot of folks got a lot of help sending their kids to school, putting money into their local communities."

"When did you last see or talk to the congressman?" Rose made notes. She knew one part of the answer from the records they had quickly reviewed.

"Day before yesterday. He called me from Washington. He wanted to talk about things." Payton's foot stopped bouncing and he sat up a little. "Jerry was a man with a mission. I can say that, knowing the man. He was righteously indignant about the corruption he saw among his colleagues and he was going to expose it as only a man like him with a distinguished war record and impeccable ethical credentials could."

Nye grunted. "Bet that didn't sit well with you."

"I speak frankly to Jerry as he does to me. I share what I think with him, and June and I told him I believed this speech would do more harm than good. It would unnecessarily make a lot of enemies of people he has to work with every day. I urged him to fix these problems through the institutions the House has created, the ethics committees. But . . . " Payton sighed heavily. "Jerry was unpersuadable."

"You worried that his speech would focus attention on you? You and him?"

"Neither of us has anything to be ashamed of, Detectives."

"Did you talk to anybody about the speech before he made it?" Rose's coldness told Nye that she hadn't gotten to his vantage point of savoring pros at the top of their game. She just didn't like Payton and didn't hide it.

"Gil Manzoni called me before Jerry to give me a heads-up. He thought the speech was a politically terrible idea. I called June and she promised to talk to Jerry. We all failed to change his mind."

"Did you know the congressman was coming back to Sacramento today?"

"It was a complete surprise."

"Didn't Manzoni or June Booker let you know?" Rose asked quickly.

"I suppose I should have said it was a complete surprise to all of us."

Nye sniffed. He debated baiting Payton about the FBI witness he and Rose were seeing in Los Angeles the next day. But since he knew so little about the witness's connection to Booker, he didn't want to give Payton a chance to react to it now. "How about Sandy Drucker? You talk to her recently?"

"No," Payton said, shaking his head. "But that's another bad idea of Jerry's I couldn't talk him out of. He's in love."

"Mrs. Booker said Drucker was blackmailing the congressman. She was threatening to end his career."

"You're joking," he said in astonishment. "June said Drucker's a blackmailer?"

"Mrs. Booker and Manzoni were trying to wrap it up yesterday," Nye said. "They didn't tell you?"

"This is the first I've heard of it," and Payton seemed genuinely amazed. "I'm stunned June never told me. I am completely at a loss."

Rose didn't let him stay lost. "Blackmailing Congressman Booker would have hit your take-home hard."

"I didn't know Jerry was being threatened. Jesus. Jesus," he murmured.

"Do you have any idea where the congressman got the money to pay for the expensive furniture and cars he bought recently?" Rose pressed again.

"I assumed it was from the house sale," Payton answered distractedly.

Nye broke in, "Nope. He bought all of that stuff before you

guys did the house deal. He have any other business interests? Stocks? Lottery winnings?"

"I don't appreciate the humor," Payton said with a wintry smile. "Jerry is an honest, dedicated public servant. There's a simple explanation for those items. It might be some windfall June got."

"You saying you didn't give him the money?"

"I never gave Jerry any money."

Nye subtly nodded to Rose, one of their signals. It was her turn to needle Payton.

"Let's assume you didn't know that the congressman was going to be in Sacramento today," she began.

"I had no idea at all. I just said so."

"Where were you today?"

Payton held his glass up, as if it would magically refill, and in a way it did. "Don't stop the freight train, Paul," Payton said. Nye watched the white-coated waiter glide away with it. "I'll give you my appointment list. You can talk to my receptionist. I had meetings all day, several over at the capitol."

"How about at the end of the day?"

"I was with five of the top executives visiting from Applied Avionics in Seattle. We were having drinks at Chops," a popular restaurant and bar across the street from the capitol, "when the news came on about Jerry. I'll give you their names."

Rose wrote them down.

Nye leaned forward. "You own any guns, Mr. Payton?"

"I never have. I couldn't see the sport side and my ex-wife was violently anti-gun."

"Not even a gun for self-protection?" Rose asked.

"I suppose I'm like Jerry. He's a fatalist. When it's your time, it's your time. No gun can change that."

Nye stood up as the waiter appeared with Payton's next drink in what was clearly going to be a long parade. This one went down in a few gulps. Give him credit, Nye acknowledged, the guy's good. You have to watch closely to see he's shook up. "Thanks, Mr. Payton. We'll have to talk again, probably tomorrow. You can help us fill in a lot of details about Congressman Booker."

"I guess"—Payton looked at Rose, as if to melt her disapproval—"what I'll miss the most is Jerry's optimism. There was always a silver lining. He had a great, rolling laugh. I don't know how June and the kids are going to cope with this. Do you remember when the truck crashed into the capitol, Detective?" He spoke to Rose.

"Yes, I do. I was called out on that one." She could have added, Like almost every other available law enforcement officer. Eight months before 9/11 a despondent truck driver rammed his tanker into the west side of the state capitol building at night while the Senate was still in session. The explosion and fire blew apart and burned almost the whole side of the building. The tanker had been filled with condensed milk. If it had been gasoline or worse, the entire building would have been obliterated and half of the legislature killed.

Payton set his glass down with great care. "I was in the Senate member's lounge and I heard the explosion and felt the entire building shudder and we all were herded to safety without knowing what had happened. I feel like that right now. Something has been tom from me and I don't know why."

Rose asked, "Do you have any idea who killed the congressman?"

"I know who did it. Terrorists. They have lists and Jerry was on their lists. I heard it on CNN tonight."

Son of a gun, Nye thought as the performance ended. I think he almost winked when he said that.

Nye and Rose got to the Peace Officers' Memorial beside the darkened Library and Courts Building. The capitol grounds across from where they stood throbbed with activity as hundreds of people were held away on L Street, filling it and snarling traffic. The crowd was unwieldy more than unruly. It seemed to have an air of expectancy.

"I don't get it, Ter," Rose said in exasperation. "The FBI's got *what* on this guy and Booker?"

"It's money, got to be. Booker's got too much he shouldn't have. Payton's his source. It's kickbacks or bribery."

"We still don't *know* that," she said again in exasperation. "I feel like I'm shadowboxing."

Nye nodded. "Here's what I'd like to figure out. I buy Payton doing something with Booker. I buy Manzoni and the wife being in on it. Maybe the girlfriend too. We got to run down this blackmail angle for sure. What I don't buy is that one of them kills him. He's the golden goose."

"How about if he was going to screw it all up for them? Then you have to tell me why Booker made his big speech if he's dirty."

"Guilty conscience?" Nye offered facetiously. "Okay. I could see the wife or Manzoni or Payton hitting him before he gives the speech. What's the percentage afterward?"

"One of them was very pissed off," Rose said.

Nye shook his head. "They're still losers and now you just committed murder. That's a double dose of bad news."

"So maybe it is terrorists." She looked at the police cars and the sheriff's department buses moving into defensive positions. "Maybe it's just a two-eleven that got screwed up, Ter."

"Yeah, come on. We missed the first meet. We're a little early for the next one. How about picking something up on the way?" He walked to their car with its Sacramento Police Department identification deliberately visible on the dashboard. "You got to admit it's kind of funny that all these clowns who were so buddy-buddy close to Booker, including the wife, didn't get told he's pulling the rug out with that speech until it's too late."

"Tell me again why he gave the speech and cut his own throat?"

"He had a lot of help with that part."

Leah tended to the conference call telephone. She dialed Zilaff. Cooper looked at his watch. She was going to report the biggest development so far. "All right. Chief Gutierrez is coming in shortly. Leah? Your news, please."

Just then Nye and Tafoya came in, unconcerned that they were late. Cooper wondered why Tafoya kept looking at her cell phone.

Leah stood. "Right now there isn't a lot of useful physical evidence. But I've just gotten the report back on the .38 bullets in Booker and Lorenz." She read off a printout from the state Department of Justice. "Both sets of bullets came from the same weapon. Without witness corroboration we didn't know until now that there was only one shooter. Now we do."

Walker glared at her, sensing that she and Cooper were holding back. "What about the gun?" he demanded.

Cooper had already gone over the weapon report with Leah. They agreed not to talk about her research on Booker until it either turned up something of value or dead-ended. If there was any valuable information, Cooper intended to leverage it in return for information from Walker. There didn't appear to be any other way to pry out whatever the FBI had developed on the congressman.

Leah read, "Manufactured in 1998, sold three times since then. The previous owners are all here in California and I'll pass around their names and addresses. The gun was reported stolen in an automobile burglary in 2002. Here's the interesting part." She looked at Cooper. "Bullets from the gun match a nonfatal shooting during a Roseville liquor store robbery in 2004. They also match a 2005 bar shooting in Santa Rosa. There were no arrests in either one."

"But now we have actual witnesses," Cooper said. "We're getting the incident reports tonight from the Roseville and Santa Rosa police. We can put the gun that killed Booker and Lorenz in someone's hands and with a physical description."

"Terrific," Walker said, although he didn't sound overly impressed. "The last time this gun shows up is over a year ago. There's no legal owner. Possession may have changed a dozen times."

"I suggest we have the police in those two jurisdictions contact the witnesses to the incidents tonight," Cooper said. "We can start finding out who had the gun last."

"Done," Walker said swiftly. "But I'm not letting us get side-tracked from the main objective."

"What is that, Agent Walker?"

"We've got to go flat-out to connect the gun with a group or person who wanted to kill Booker because he was a member of Congress." He added as an afterthought, "Or eliminate that possibility."

At that moment, Nye laconically chimed in. "Maybe you ought to think about blackmail. Tafoya and I got two people who say Booker was being blackmailed."

"We're looking at every credible angle for the shooting," Walker said. "But the terrorist possibility comes first."

Cooper shook his head at Nye and Tafoya, who both looked a little disgusted. Like the other cops, and probably the FBI agents in the command center, the first solid information about the shooting was the stolen gun. It was a rookie mistake to latch on to a hypothesis like terrorists so early. But, Cooper recalled, Walker had emphatically pointed out that this was not an ordinary shooting. Other exigencies, generated by the times, were distorting the investigation.

The remainder of the meeting went quickly.

Walker toyed with an empty paper coffee cup. "Zilaff and my team are starting a triage through the records from Manzoni's office and the Booker home office. We're looking for a pattern of transactions. I've got agents securing access to the bank records for Booker, his wife, Manzoni, Sandra Drucker, and Ralph Payton."

Zilaff said, "I think I can find loans from Payton to June Booker as part of other financial activity. They're showing up as fees or management costs."

Walker went on, "We've got teams working through the National Security Agency and the CIA to put together all the people they've been monitoring in this area, Lodi, Stockton, greater Sacramento. We'll start interviews in the morning. We're also coordinating with federal Homeland Security about people entering the country in the last few months. We're going through the various claims of responsibility for the killing." He glanced at a paper. "Now up to five for connections to anybody in the country."

Leah whispered to Cooper, "The media will go running after the terrorist connection."

"Not much we can do about it," he agreed. Interviewing suspects, investigating foreign organizations would be very visible. Checking bank records for a lobbyist or the dead man's wife would not. Everyone was keenly aware that the national threat level had been raised to red in the last hour.

Cooper sat down beside Leah. He was tired but she was hitting her stride. Sometimes he thought she operated on batteries. Maybe more coffee would help him for the next few hours. Detective Drier went over the expanding examination of Jamie Lorenz's acquaintances and coworkers, tracking down anybody who disliked him for any reason. The recital was a sad one. Lorenz had been through four jobs in six years, engaged to be married, and then that fell apart. He was planning to go back to college. He was struggling to change his life at the moment he picked up Congressman Gerald Booker at the airport that afternoon.

Tafoya in detail efficiently laid out the meetings with Manzoni, June Booker, and Payton. She kept glancing at her cell phone as she talked. Cooper assigned her and Nye to reinterview all three when they got back from Los Angeles.

"Here's Chief Gutierrez," Cooper said as Tafoya finished. He stepped aside as the police chief strode in, followed by his two senior deputy chiefs.

"I'm not going to take up your time for long," he said, fatigue tingeing his brisk tone. "I've just finished a meeting with the mayor, representatives from the governor's office, the county Board of Supervisors. The message to me was loud and clear. They want answers tomorrow. Which means I want answers tomorrow. I'm doing a video press conference with your boss"— he cocked his head at Walker—"and the attorney general at ten A.M. I intend to have something to say."

Cooper folded his arms. Nye and Tafoya listened with professional courtesy. They know what's coming and I don't think it will change how they do their jobs in the coming hours or days, he thought.

"I can't speak for the AG or your boss," the chief said to Cooper and Leah, "but my detectives and line officers know the score tonight. Bring me something solid tomorrow or you're out." He grimly smiled at the faces he knew around the table, lingering on Nye. "I'll be right behind you."

He left and the meeting broke up after Cooper said they would reconvene at eight. Nye and Tafoya stopped Walker. "We're on a zero dark thirty flight to LA tomorrow," Rose said to him. "Can you give us a little more help here? Who this witness is? How she ties in?"

Cooper and Leah had come up, files under their arms. "How about telling them if she's connected to Payton?"

Walker was opaque. "Do your usual good police work. You've got a lot of background now. I'm sure you and DAs Cooper and Fisher will pretty quickly come up with interesting notions we can all toss around."

He left. Leah said, "This is the wink-and-nod method of dealing with the FBI. Plausible deniability in case Walker ever gets asked about what he told us or when."

Cooper saw Rose Tafoya worriedly checking her cell phone again. "Something wrong?" he asked.

"Problem at home. I'll handle it."

"I'm on it with her," Nye said. It had not escaped Cooper that the much older detective was more than normally protective of his partner. Given the circumstances, that could be admirable or hazardous. It might be a temptation to cover for her or put himself at risk in a dangerous situation. He hoped Nye was aware of what he was doing.

"All right. Have a safe flight." He smiled. "I'm sure the Roseville and Santa Rosa police will turn up enough to keep everybody happy for a little while."

"I ain't worried," Nye said and they left, talking.

Leah walked back to her office with Cooper. "I didn't want

to get your hopes up, Denny, but I think I've found something in a couple of old rap sheet entries."

"Booker?"

"More than him. Let me dig down. I may have to go out to the archives in the morning if I need to look at the original case files."

"Now I'm very curious." He stifled a yawn. "I've got to get some coffee if we're going to keep going tonight. You want some?"

"No, I'm fine." She had already turned her attention to the pages spread thickly over her desk.

"I know you are," he said with affection.

THIRTEEN

COOPER AND LEAH GOT HOME a little before two A.M. He felt sluggish and fuzzy-minded, but she brought files and other work from the investigation with her. He was, he admitted, a little resentful of her endless energy.

She dropped the files in the small dining room and went back to their bedroom. Cooper wearily took off his coat, leaving it on a chair in the living room, took off his tie and left it on the kitchen table, and rolled up his sleeves. Except for Leah opening drawers and moving around in the bedroom, the house and the neighborhood were dark and quiet. He went out the kitchen door and stood on the cracked concrete steps leading to the backyard and its stripling pear and apple trees they had planted over the summer. The neighborhood was older, tree-shaded, and mostly single-story homes with compact front lawns and backyards. They had block parties for the Fourth of July and a painful ritual of going door to door singing carols at Christmas. Other than that, he didn't really mix very much with his neighbors, although everyone waved or made idle and short small talk if he ran into them washing the car or boat, mowing the grass, keeping an eye on the few small children playing outside. Leah knew more of the people nearby than he did. It was an aging, settled neighborhood and it lay quiet and prone tonight under the cloud-striped sky and the half-moon glittering bonily above it.

What's coming? Cooper wondered. He crossed his arms. The air was already signaling a cold winter ahead. His neighbors and millions of people across the country lay sleeping and dreaming. Right now it was a night of uncertainties and anxieties, rivalries between federal and state law enforcement agencies, personal animosities, and numberless open questions. Later that day, the demands for quick answers, simple solutions would come thick and fast and unstoppable. He fervently wished he had some answers. What was the FBI holding back about Booker and why? Was there an informant tied up in it all, as Leah believed? Did the FBI know whether Booker had been the target of an assassin, the victim of a random crime, or was he killed by someone close to him, his wife, Manzoni, his chief of staff, Ralph Payton, his friend and benefactor, or even his mistress Sandy Drucker?

Cooper quizzically studied the dark homes beyond his own. Then there were the questions about Booker himself. If he was taking money from Payton or someone else, why give a very public speech denouncing exactly what he was doing? It was suicide and everything Cooper had learned in the last eight hours about Congressman Booker pointed away from a man who had a death wish, either personal or political. But he did give the speech and made a lot of news instantly.

Leah came up beside him and put her arm around him.

"What's up?" she asked.

"Thinking about the investigation. Thinking about Booker. He doesn't make sense to me."

She had changed into a T-shirt and plain gray sweatpants, her hair combed loosely, and she was barefoot. She looked shadowed and vibrantly alive in the faint moonlight. Like she's on the hunt, he thought. Loving every minute of it.

"I think Booker was a man who wanted out."

"Of what?"

"I don't know. Maybe everything. His career, his marriage, the way he spent every day. He had Drucker and he knew that was dangerous and everybody around him must have been pounding him to get rid of her all the time. He made a speech yesterday"—she smiled ruefully—"day before yesterday now. He was daring the FBI or a reporter to ask questions about him. Shine a light on him."

"The FBI already has some answers."

"I think that makes my point. I'll bet he knew they were checking him out."

They turned and went back into the kitchen. It was brightly and warmly papered in yellow, the refrigerator and microwave were new with their occupancy, but the oven and the dishwasher were almost antiques. Dishes from breakfast still lay in the sink. He and Leah hadn't sorted out a lot of daily diligences like that, and sometimes neither of them attended to things so that there would be a weekend of frenzied cleaning that left them vowing to avoid doing it again.

"What prompts these insights about our victim?" Cooper asked, opening the refrigerator and unhappily inspecting the few items inside.

"A couple things. He was a risk taker, hotdog pilot. He played to win, that's what Nye and Tafoya got from Manzoni. I think he was playing out his own very risky game plan."

Cooper took out sliced meat and mayonnaise. "If he was compromised by Payton, why not just resign from Congress?"

"Booker did things his way," Leah said, opening a cupboard and almost randomly grabbing a can of beef stew. "If he was looking for an exit from everything, I think he'd do it with a big bang and cleanly."

"Pull the temple down behind him?"

"Burn every bridge," she said, the whine of the electric can opener blurring her words. "Any other cliches you know?"

Cooper stared unhappily at what he proposed to eat. "I suppose not. What are you having, something hot or cold?"

"Sort of hot." She showed him the can as she dumped it into a bowl and shoved that into the microwave.

"Can we share?"

"No."

"No?"

"Well, all right." She watched the microwave.

He got one of the sturdy pottery soup bowls that Leah had contributed down from the cupboard. "Did you find anything in Booker's record?"

"I'm definitely going to make a trip out to Records in the morning. There's an old rap sheet on him in the system, just a notation of a traffic violation, no dispo. There's another case number listed, but I can't locate it. I'm going to find the case file, if there is one after all this time."

"That's a little odd," he said, but the vagaries of the police and sheriff's departments' record keeping were a problem they dealt with too often as prosecutors. The omissions and flaws were more apparent in older cases before computerized indexing. "How old is it?"

"Twenty years." She inhaled steam rising from the stew as she took it out of the microwave. "The missing in action case number has my curiosity going. I don't think the traffic deal is really important."

"Not after twenty years," he said dryly. "I don't see much connection to what we need to find out immediately. Don't spend much time on it." He gently took the bowl and roughly split the stew between her and him. He spooned some back into her bowl. "There we go. A really fine dining experience at the end of a hard day."

She started eating and walking to the living room. "I'm going to work on the witness statements for a while before I go to bed, Denny."

"Okay, I'm just going to bed," he said, blowing on a spoonful of stew to cool it. It would be wonderful if there was something valuable in the collection of statements the city cops had turned in from witnesses who knew Booker and June or Drucker or who had been around 1820 N at the time of the shooting.

They had found three passing motorists who saw the cab pull up. But there was still, maddeningly, no one who saw the actual shooting.

The most fruitful line of investigation lay in the .38 gun and its prior owners and the subsequent crimes in which it had been used.

The problem, he thought, chewing slowly and tiredly, was time. There was so little time.

Nye sat on the edge of his bed in the dark for a few moments. It was a little after two A.M. He massaged his left knee, which had started making odd crackling sounds and aching recently, like the bolts and strings were coming apart. I am so far out of warranty too, he thought.

He stood up. He tried to remember when he had slept through the night last and could not. What about last Thanksgiving? He had spent it with his daughter and her family and they had eaten so much he fell asleep in front of their TV watching football. Since then it was a clockwork routine almost like a job itself, up at two, up again at four, finally up at six or so, and then breakfast and off to work.

He switched on the light. On the wall opposite his bed hung the picture he liked best of the family, taken when the kids were just eight and ten and he and Marceen seemed to have things between them at least under control if not actually swell. He remembered having the picture taken on the spur of the moment at Kmart when they were shopping for school supplies. Marceen was actually smiling at him.

He scratched his leg and walked barefoot into the kitchen. The funny thing was that after he stopped drinking it was as if his head lit up or sparked and just kept buzzing even when he should be asleep. It was very unnerving.

He and Marceen had moved to a smaller house when the kids left, and when she left it struck him as too big. Too many rooms. Too many things to keep track of. He stopped in the kitchen, turning on the old-fashioned overhead light. He debated on a glass of milk and settled for a pull of water from the sink's faucet. He wiped his mouth and on an impulse that had been vaguely bothering him since he got home, he went to the old Princess model telephone on the wall and dialed.

Rose answered almost on the first ring.

"Hey, Rosie," he said, keeping his voice whispery for some reason, "I forgot if we agreed that I pick you up in the morning or you pick me up to go to the airport." It was a lie. They had very specifically agreed to meet at five thirty at his house and he would drive.

"Ter," she said without rancor, "are you checking up on me?"

"No. I just forgot. I didn't want to waste time in the morning when we got a plane to catch."

"Look, I'm fine. I'll be at your place at five thirty."

"Yeah, great. That's all I needed." Then he quickly said, "But everything is okay, right?"

"No," she said softly. "Luis didn't come home. He picked Annorina up this afternoon and left her here alone." The words were still soft but bitter and angry. "She knows the drill, she locked the doors, pulled the shades, and waited for me to come home."

"Christ," he said. "I'm sorry to hear that."

"He'll come home sometime soon and we'll have a good fight about it again in the morning and then I'll see you."

"I can talk to him, Rosie."

"I know you could," she chuckled quietly. "I got to work this out myself, Ter. This is my family."

"I'm here if you need me."

"Well . . . " She paused. "I like knowing that."

She hung up. He flipped off the light in the kitchen and went into the living room. He had sprung for cable TV last year, an extravagance that made less and less sense every month because he watched so little TV as it was. He thought he'd surf around all those channels and maybe find something that would stop the buzzing in his head. Then he realized he'd keep running into the endless loop of news stories about Booker's shooting and terrorists and talking heads getting more worked up.

So he got as far as the old blue sofa and its familiar worn spots from the kids or the short-lived Great Dane they had owned for a few years. He sat down in the dark and thought about what he had once had and now did not and what Rose had and might lose.

Nye swore several times without being fully aware he was doing it.

He thought of Rose and a dead congressman and anthills.

Sometime later, Cooper stirred when he felt Leah crawl into bed beside him. She lay close, her breath soft on the back of his neck.

He started awake later when the phone jangled on the small table on his side of the bed. Leah moved, half asleep and half awake. He grabbed the phone.

"Dennis Cooper?" the husky-voiced woman on the line asked, mariachi music almost drowning her out.

"Who is it?" he said. He got calls at odd times, as Leah did, from police agencies sometimes. But this didn't sound like a cop wanting to run facts by him about a warrant for someone they needed to pick up immediately or whether they had enough to arrest someone connected to a homicide.

"This is Sandy Drucker," she said more loudly. "I've got to talk to you right now."

"About what?" he asked, Leah awake and pressing close to hear.

"I want to tell you about Jerry and what's going on. He deserves to have his side of the story heard," Sandy said.

"All right," he said calmly. "I need to let the FBI know—" and she cut him off.

"I called you. I want to tell you, not the FBI."

"Where are you?"

"Across the river in Broderick. Do you know where the 321 Club is? Come over the Tower Bridge, follow the road into West Sacramento," and she gave him directions.

"I'll find it. Let me give you my cell number," and he slowly did it twice. "Give me about twenty minutes," he said.

"I'm trusting you, Mr. Cooper. I can help you but I can just disappear too."

"I want to hear what you have to say, Ms. Drucker."

The mariachi trumpeting surged and then the line went dead.

Cooper got out of bed and started to get dressed in jeans and a sweater. Leah got up too. "I heard the last bits," she said. "Sounds like Drucker's staying away from 1820 N."

"Yes, it does. I think she's going to run." He put on his gym shoes and a tweed sport coat. "She's a better source for Booker's actions in the last few days than the others close to him."

"I should come with you, Denny. You need a witness when you talk to her."

He knew that Leah was right. It was rarely wise to interview a witness or a suspect without a second cop or DA present. People had a habit of forgetting what they said, denying they said things, or miraculously coming up with an entirely different set of facts and explanations.

"I know," he said, grabbing his wallet and car keys. "Drucker's on the edge. She really does want to tell us something about Booker, but she's spooked. I have to see her alone."

"Then it could be a waste of time, Denny."

"It's a judgment call." He grinned. "Maybe it's one of the good ones."

Cooper had not been out at that hour in the morning for a long time and he had forgotten the weird ghostly feeling Sacramento had after midnight. As he drove over the gold-painted Tower Bridge, only its red airplane warning lights blinking, the spectral quality of the city was very strong. It was as if it was a set or stage, empty and unreal. All of the black office buildings and government monuments seemed insubstantial and made of smoke. Along the Sacramento River the brush was dark, tangled, and primeval. The night was silent.

There was no traffic as he crossed the bridge and sped onto Broderick just over the county line, a small mostly working-class Hispanic city right against Sacramento, merging with it seamlessly. He thought of the cases he'd done over the years involving that deceptively swift-flowing river. Victims dumped down the embankment or from the levee roads, victims in boxes or tarps, victims in their cars, a bullet in the head, the elderly couple in a murder-suicide pact, holding hands in their half-submerged Acura.

He passed through the city and down the levee road. After a few minutes he saw ahead the only lights anywhere except for a few stray office monoliths back across the river in Sacramento. He pulled into the muddy parking lot beside the 321 Club. Tall elms and Chinese oaks hung over the stucco and brick building and its flat tin roof. Neon Mexican beer signs flickered in the windows and the rhythm of mariachis floated out.

Cooper looked around inside. There were people at the Formica-topped bar, three men loudly arguing in Spanish, two women giggling and throwing down the last of a pitcher of margaritas. A young man with only a stubble of hair on his head was precariously stuck on a bar stool, his head propped on one hand, his mouth open and eyes closed.

Wooden booths with brown-plastic-covered seats took up most of the club. Over everything was the smell of frying oil and *carnitas* and the music. He looked for Sandy Drucker.

He found her sitting in a booth near the kitchen. She had five beer bottles on the table and a half-empty plastic basket of tortilla chips. He sat down opposite her.

"Hello, Ms. Drucker," Cooper said, "how are you?"

"In an odd place, to be perfectly candid, Mr. Cooper." She was bright-eyed but haunted. "Can we go right to Sandy and Dennis?"

"Fine with me." He was going to let her drive the conversation. She had the compulsion to talk and he didn't want to impede it.

"Well, I'm in an odd place, as I said. I feel a little like there's an explosion just behind my eyes and I can't quite see everything anymore. I've tried drinking." She indicated the bottles. "And I've tried crying. I'll probably do that again while we're talking. But nothing's quite working." She looked at him imploringly. "What do you think it means?"

"You've had a terrific shock," Cooper said. "It takes a while to adjust to what happened to Jerry. I've dealt with a lot of people who go through what you're going through. Most of the time it gets easier."

"Not always, though, right? Sometimes it stays just like this, like life stopped at a particular moment and in a particular place."

"Yes," he admitted. "Sometimes it never gets easier. But I think you're one of the survivors."

"You bet I am," she said. She tried to sound defiant even though she was miserable and frightened. "You're part of my survival package, Dennis. What they did to Jerry, they're not going to do to me because you'll know the truth."

Cooper had perfected a sympathetic face, part pose and part genuine, but intended to elicit information. "What did happen to him?"

Sandy desultorily poked among the chips. "He was murdered."

"Do you know who killed him?"

"The people who were bribing him. Ralph Payton's clients or maybe Payton himself or he hired someone. It all comes back to the same people. Jerry took money from people Ralph Payton wanted him to."

"How do you know he was being bribed?"

"The last six months, Jerry was very upset. He wanted me to know what he had done and what he was being forced to do at that instant. It made him sick. He didn't want secrets between us."

"Did he give you names, specific people who were giving him money?"

"I wrote them down for you." She smiled bleakly. "I assumed you'd want them." She reached into the handbag beside her and gave him a neatly folded piece of paper.

He quickly ran down the unfamiliar names and companies, listed in a firm longhand. Walker and the FBI must have names, but he might not have all of them, Cooper reasoned. Drucker had given him the means to force the FBI back to working together on the investigation.

She spoke as he read. "Jerry's tragedy, Dennis, is that he always wanted to be a good guy. He wanted to do the right thing and he wanted people to look up to him. I did." She cried, head shaking slightly back and forth.

"Did he tell you why he gave that speech if he was taking bribes?" Cooper put the list in his pocket.

She wiped her nose and eyes with a crumpled paper napkin. "He was tired of June's threats, the way his life had turned out, I think. Jerry and I talked every day and we spent as much time together as we could when he came back to California to visit his district. You see what had happened?" She stared down, then looked at Cooper. "Jerry was taking money from aerospace companies that had legislation in front of his committee. He voted the way they asked. Or he put things in the Congressional Record that would help a particular company. A few times he said things that would slam a rival."

"How long had the bribery been going on, Sandy?"

"For about the last three years, I guess. He was taking much more since he and I got together. June was behind that. You know she was the model for all those Valley Ale calendars about twenty years ago? She's the 'Valley Ale Girl' popping out of a very low-cut Western barmaid's outfit. I think she tried to buy all the calendars and pretend they didn't exist. Not something the wife of a respected congressman wants lying around. I think there's a lot more she did she'd like to pretend didn't happen. Anyway, she was ripping strips off the walls at home, he told me, she was so furious he was seeing me. Her price was more. More cars, more jewelry, more everything. Jerry paid her price."

"Mrs. Booker told our detectives tonight that you were blackmailing the congressman, taking money and threatening to destroy his political career."

"Me blackmailing Jerry?" she asked incredulously. "I didn't take any money from him. June was the one who demanded he get them into a bigger house and start making some real money from his seniority in Congress. Christ. *She* was blackmailing him, telling him she'd leave him, let everybody know he was an adulterer. That would make her the victim and he'd be ruined."

Cooper needed to know how frank Drucker could be. Her value as a source or a witness later depended on it. If she was involved in Booker's murder, it was vital to test whatever she said. "What about your condo on N Street, Sandy? Your salary as a lawyer with the Legislative Counsel doesn't come near the cost of it."

"Jerry insisted he pay for part of the condo at 1820 N. We were living there together, he said, so that was only fair. It made being together more real. So, I did take something from him and that was wrong." She nodded. "After Jerry and I had been living together for a while, I knew where the money came from. He told me what he was doing. I realized that everyone gets offered a bribe sometime. Some people take it. Sometimes it's a new car, house, college for the kids, sex, drugs, money. But sooner or later, everyone gets a bribe shoved at them. I know that sounds horribly cynical. If you look at it a little differently, it's not as bad. It's a favor. It's a bond. I let Jerry pay for part of the condo because that brought us closer. I suppose it's only a rationalization for doing what I knew was wrong. But I did it."

Cooper sat back in the booth. "Did Jerry tell you who knew he was taking payoffs from these companies?"

"Manzoni and June orchestrated it. Payton brought the company executives and Jerry together and got a fee. The problem was how blatant it was getting, Jerry said. June wanted more money, Payton wanted more for his clients. The whole house sale between June and Jerry and Payton was a flat-out payoff for a major contract award to Applied Avionics for a new jet fighter navigation system last year. Jerry steered it through his committee."

"All of this income is reportable," Cooper said. "Did Jerry tell you how the bribes were being hidden?"

"He used to tell me that Payton would say, 'there's reportable and then there's reportable.' Payton had come up with some scheme to launder the bribes so they looked like something else, came from someone else, and would be innocuous if anyone looked at Jerry's tax returns or his outside income reports."

"Have you talked to the FBI?"

"Bastards," she said vehemently. "They were the reason Jerry was so upset. They were calling him or his staff. He said Payton was very mad because he was getting calls too and agents would come to his office in Washington. People were already starting to talk and Jerry knew it would get worse."

"The FBI knew about Jerry's deals with aerospace companies?"

"He thought so."

"Did he tell you how they found out?"

"No." She shook her head, and the music ended abruptly, leaving only loud chatter at the bar and the thud of the young man's head hitting the bar when his hand slid out from under him. "I think they had a source, somebody who was feeding them information. I suppose it could have been June or Manzoni or Payton if they were worried about what might happen to them, but it could be somebody at one of the companies too. Or Jerry's staff." She cried again silently. "He was so sad and unhappy near the end, and then a couple of days ago when he decided to blow it all up with that speech, it was like he was the old Jerry, ready to slay the dragons, wanting to make it a better world."

"Do you know if he told his wife or any of the others that he was coming back to Sacramento right after giving the speech?"

"Just the opposite. He called me from Dulles, just before he took off. He sounded like a kid, very pleased he was getting away without anybody knowing it. We made a date for yesterday evening, like we were starting over. He was going to leave June, he said. The FBI would come after him and that was it for his congressional career." She smiled shyly. "We actually first met on a flight back to Sacramento. It was a pure accident. We were sitting together and he spilled a little vodka on me when we hit some turbulence and we started talking and we went on talking until yesterday."

"I'm sorry," Cooper said sincerely. The loneliness he had initially sensed in Sandy Drucker rolled off her in invisible waves. He thought she was one of those people who didn't commit often in the course of their days, but when they did it was irrevocable. Then suddenly her life with Booker ended violently. She was shaken beyond what she ever imagined. "I think you should go home, Sandy. I can drive you. I'll have a Sacramento police officer nearby for you."

"I can't go near the condo," she spat. "It's going to be a tourist attraction and I'll be the one they try to feed peanuts. Oh no. I'm leaving. I tried to get out tonight and I'm sorry I hit one of your officers. That was uncalled for. I'm very scared, Dennis. I don't mind admitting it. Jerry tried to start over and he was killed. I don't intend to let that happen to me. So I'll go far away and bury myself some place new and maybe I will survive after all," she said, nodding to herself.

"I could arrest you for that assault on Detective Tafoya," Cooper said. "You can help us find whoever killed Jerry. You need to stay here."

She eyed him analytically. "I've thought about it a great, great deal, Dennis. Do you know why Jerry was murdered like that, out in the open a couple of blocks from the state capitol?"

"What do you think?"

"It was a message, a billboard with flashing lights." She traced the air with her hands. "Jerry Booker got his. He broke the rules. He went public. I think you should be focusing on Payton. He has a lot of clients and Jerry crippled Payton's business. Take a look at those clients."

"I don't think it was terrorists, Sandy. Beyond that, everything's wide open."

She wiped her eyes again because she had been silently crying. At the bar two men were trying to rouse the young man lying facedown. "The last time I saw Jerry, we stayed in, had dinner. He was drinking and he turned off the light in the kitchen and stood in the dark. Then he came into the living room where it was light. He asked me, how could you tell who was good or evil? Who was in the light or the dark? He went and stood halfway between the two rooms. What am I now? he asked me. A good man or a bad one? And the solemn, dreadful truth is I don't know, Dennis. Poor Jerry was like me and the rest of us, half in the light and half in the dark, and he hated that."

She stood.

"Don't leave Sacramento, Sandy," Cooper said, getting up too.

"I've got to." She smoothed her skirt and looked around the club. "They're not getting me like they did Jerry."

"I'll get you protection, Sandy."

"My best protection is to disappear."

Cooper walked with her to the door and out into the muddy parking lot. "I'll have to notify the FBI and the police."

"Please," she answered, imploringly again, staring at him. "Jerry was holding something important back and I think he was going to tell me yesterday. Maybe he found out who was helping the FBI, I don't know. I do know he's dead and I have to save myself now." She said nothing more but quickly got into a small foreign car and gunned it out of the parking lot, lurching up the slight incline onto the levee road and speeding away. Cooper noted the license number and the vehicle description and on his way back into Sacramento, he checked with the police that Drucker was indeed still driving her own car. He told them the direction she was heading. He called and left a message on Walker's voice mail. Then he drove home, into the ghostly city waiting for a strange and frightening new day, and he wondered, as he had occasionally during his years as a prosecutor, where he stood in the light or the shadows.

"We shouldn't arrest her," Leah said. "She'll bail without too much trouble and when we get to trial on Booker's case, Drucker's credibility is thin."

"If we get to trial," he said. He drank the warm whiskey and lemon she'd made for them both, a sovereign remedy for nerves and sleeplessness.

"Trust me. We will."

"I love your sunny optimism," he said tiredly. "You're right about her. I just want to locate her and make sure she's safe."

Leah finished her drink, rinsed the glass. "Going through the witness statements tonight makes it pretty clear the shootings were very fast. If it was a two-eleven, the shooter didn't say anything. The witnesses line up to the second almost. Just before the shootings. Just after. Except we don't have anyone who saw the shootings or the shooter."

Cooper drained his glass and left it on the table. "Talk about perfect timing."

Leah went with him to the bedroom, switching off lights. "I don't know, Denny. I think it means that the shooter killed Lorenz and Booker and just walked on, like nothing had happened. I think he simply faded into the scenery and that's why nobody noticed anything."

"Oh, swell," he said. "That sounds more like a hit than a robbery."

FOURTEEN

AT FIVE FORTY-FIVE IN THE morning, a puffy-eyed Nye and a sharply turned-out Rose Tafoya stood in the security line slowly snaking its way into the boarding gate area at Sacramento Metropolitan Airport. Nye groused again.

"I can't believe these chumps didn't let us bring our guns. Who the hell do they think we are? Who the hell do *we* look like?"

Rose shook her head. "New rule, you heard, Ter. Everybody's got the jumps."

Nye was not appeased. "Chumps. We're a couple of cops, for Christ's sake. We look like a couple of cops. They could've gotten Ph.D.s the way they studied our goddamn department IDs."

"Look around," she said. "It didn't take long to put it all back," and she gestured at the green-uniformed National Guardsmen all around the terminal with rifles and their quiet, alert dogs. The men were pale and cold under the bright lights. "You hear people talking much? It's like going to church. So don't sweat it."

Nye sourly finished his cup of airport coffee, the stuff he got from the regular snack counter, not one of the franchise places scattered everywhere. He knew he was making a nod to reverse snobbery. It was quieter than he recalled at the airport, but he'd chalked that up to the unholy hour of the morning. Now he looked around at the blank, forced-calm faces in the line and he thought Rose was right. Fear, oppressive and roiling just beneath the surface, was everywhere.

"They're still chumps," he said as the line slowly inched forward. The ordeal of the metal detector and search was to come. "Some knucklehead starts patting me down," and he ominously left it unfinished.

"You'll just smile like everybody and if he gets too friendly you ask him to buy you a drink."

"Ha, ha," he said. "You telling me you honestly don't mind giving up your piece?"

"We'll pick them up on the return leg, I told you. Anyway, we'll be okay just for today without them. We're in LA, we're going to see a civilian witness. It'll be fine," she said. They were near the head of the line. She started opening her coat to put it on the conveyor belt into the X-ray machine. "Nothing's going to happen, okay? We're going to Hancock Park, we're going to the Japanese Consulate." She had tracked down the witness late yesterday.

"Yeah, yeah. Why's our mystery witness at the consulate?" He was grumpily shucking off his overcoat.

"It's the emperor's birthday party," she said with a grin.

Leah was waiting for the short, pudgy sergeant when he drove up just before eight o'clock in his old Chevy. He had wisps of fine white hair and he sucked noisily on a breath freshener.

"I'm your first customer," she said, showing him her DA identification.

"Well, you sure ain't the last," he grunted and unlocked the plain heavy metal gray door. The records of the Sacramento

Police Department and the district attorney had been consolidated for economy in a large warehouse some years earlier. There was not, and, Leah assumed, would never be, money available to scan the millions of pages of old files into an electronic format. So they sat in a marginally climate-controlled large concrete building in an industrial part of the city, surrounded by furniture manufacturers, tool shops, and auto part suppliers.

She was anxious to get inside, partly because it was a chilly, bright blue October morning. But mostly because it was a little like opening presents on Christmas day. She always looked forward to the opening, not the gift itself. It was the pursuit that excited her in a case, not the conviction really. She wondered, as she told Denny the day before, if there was anything left after twenty years, or if there was, if she could find it.

And she didn't have much time to spend here. He was right to make this a quick side trip.

"Well, come on, come on," the sergeant said. "Let me get my coat off and get the coffee started and show me what you need."

Leah tamped down her impatience and after a few minutes, she gave him the case numbers she had and Booker's name, hoping that there was more of a tracking system in the records themselves than in the case information available online. The old sergeant stood behind a counter, accessible only through a locked grille metal door.

He perched a pair of bifocals down his large nose and slowly pecked into a computer terminal. He seemed to be the only person in the records building.

"Well, here we go," and he started jotting down numbers. "I'll go take a look, but it's kind of thin—" and she interrupted.

"Look, why don't you let me do that? I know my way around files."

"Nobody's allowed back there but authorized staff. That's me."

"I hear your coffee," she said. "Get a cup, come on back, and take a look in a couple of minutes and make sure I'm not messing things up."

"I can sign files out," he said stubbornly. "I can't let you go poking around."

"It will save you a lot of time if you let me take a look," she said. "This is the Booker investigation. *We're* short of time."

"Yeah, I know. The big ones are always in a hurry." He seemed right on the edge of giving her permission. She thought an appeal to generosity might do the trick.

"Could you bring me a cup of coffee when you come back?" she asked quickly. "I didn't get a chance to get one before I rushed over here."

"I could do that," he said, brightening a little. "Okay. Here's the aisle and stack numbers. The old files have red and blue tabs on the sides, so you should be able to catch the name."

"Thanks," Leah said gratefully as the grille door opened with an electrical buzz.

"You take cream and sugar or just sugar? You look like a cream and sugar to me."

Cooper and Walker walked up the stone steps of the capitol, passing through rings of troops and police that closed off the building. The initial crowd nearby had dispersed overnight, leaving a hardy core camped out around the barricaded perimeter. But people were already starting to gather in large numbers.

Cooper had told Walker about his meeting with Sandy Drucker. "Booker was pretty open about taking bribes," Cooper said. "Here's the list," and he handed Walker a copy of what Drucker had given him. "Do they ring any bells?" he asked with a trace of sarcasm.

Walker ran down the list. "If someone took a look at Ralph Payton's clients and cross-referenced it with business-class trips Booker took and some major contributions he got, they might find these names."

Workmen were putting the last nails and drapery on a stark catafalque set on the rotunda just to the side of the statue of

Queen Isabella of Spain that dumpily sat in the center of the marble floor. Overhead, very far above on the inside of the dome, was the colorfully dramatic painting of various great events in the state's history. "You knew Booker was being bought, Agent Walker. You've been looking at him for a while, I'm sure."

"Neither confirm nor deny, Cooper. That's the talking point I was given."

Cooper didn't think the FBI would acknowledge the accuracy of Drucker's information. But Walker didn't dispute it either, and in the strange language of deniability he was speaking, the silence was as good as an agreement Drucker had it right.

"She also said Booker was holding something back in the last couple of days. She thought it was something he badly wanted to tell her."

"He was going back to his wife."

"No, he was happy to be making a clean break," Cooper said. "What do you think he was reluctant to tell Sandy?"

"I really don't know." Walker's expression tightened over the hammering and whirring of electric drills. "Booker had a guilty conscience. He spilled his guts to the world and maybe he was going to show Drucker two tickets to Belize."

"Why Belize?"

"Why not? I went there last year for the scuba. Great clear water, Cooper." He turned from the catafalque. "We're looking for her. You shouldn't have let her go," and the words were harsh without raising his voice.

"I couldn't stop her. We can't arrest her without shooting ourselves in the process. She needs to be an untainted witness."

"When we find her again," Walker said, facing Cooper angrily. "I've got twenty-six agents arriving at the airport in an hour. First job is finding Drucker. The second one is finding whoever had the .38 S and W last."

"SPD just sent over what they got from the Santa Rosa and Roseville cops." Cooper had noted the most important items on the printout he took from his coat pocket. "The good news is that it looks like both the 2004 and 2005 crimes were committed by the same person. Male, black adult, about twenty-five to thirty. Medium height, one-sixty to one-eighty. Wearing jeans, a black hooded sweatshirt."

"I can see why they didn't close either of the offenses. That description stinks."

Cooper put the printout in his pocket. "As far as it goes. But at least one witness said the suspect was missing two fingers on his left hand." He held his own up and wiggled the fingers. "The Roseville cops developed a very good suspect, but he had an equally good alibi."

"Like what?"

"He was in county jail when both crimes were committed. He was doing six months on his third auto burg and possession of a controlled substance. Meth, I think."

Walker checked his watch. "I need to go meet my agents and talk to Zilaff again. Sounds like the .38 is still cold and we'll need to run it down."

They turned along the marble halls, passing the mounted display cases filled with artifacts peculiar to each of California's fifty-eight counties. Farther on, crisply uniformed Highway Patrol officers guarded the large double doors to the governor's office. Added to their detail were two National Guardsmen, each armed with an AK-47.

Cooper had wanted to see the preparations for the congressman's one-day lying-in-state. The official ceremony was scheduled to begin at five P.M. and the featured players would be the governor and June Booker. It would be a window on the public mood. Most people, except in his district, had never heard of Jerry Booker before his killing. As a martyr or a symbol he might be used to inflame people or frighten them.

"We can develop something on the gun, Agent Walker, fairly quickly."

"How?"

"The suspect with the solid alibi has two brothers, and all three brothers are about the same age. If the lone witness knew one or more of the brothers, he could have made a mistake about who he saw pointing a gun at him and assumed he saw the brother with missing fingers. The local cops had no compelling reason to pursue an investigation that looked like it was at a dead end. I had another homicide with this kind of mistaken identification a few years ago."

"Okay," Walker agreed. "That's a reasonable starting point." He glanced at Cooper. "Do you mind a personal question?"

"I don't know. Go ahead."

"Do you like you what you do?"

"Very much," Cooper said. Long ago he had realized that being a prosecutor satisfied a basic need in him. It was the only way, however tedious or faulty on occasion, to find order in human affairs. It was a way, he thought lately, of avoiding the nightmarish possibility that there was no order and no justice.

"I like what I do a lot too," Walker said. "So I guess we both have to figure out a way to make sure we don't cut each other off. Like your chief of police said last night, short straws are going out the door."

"It's almost time for his press conference. You can watch it back at my office." They were nearly at the end of the long corridor. Cooper wanted to test Walker's tentatively offered olive branch.

"I've got one question, Agent Walker," he said. "Sandy Drucker believes you've had an informant helping you gather evidence against Booker. If you do have an informant, whoever that is goes high on the list of suspects."

Walker slowed. "Same rule, unfortunately, Cooper. I can't confirm or deny. I can say that any informant, *if* there is an informant, can't possibly be a suspect."

"You know that answer's unacceptable."

"I suppose I do. You'll have to trust me."

Most major TV stations carried the press conference. Cooper stood, arms folded, with Walker slowly pacing around the conference table in Joyce Gutherie's fourth-floor office. On the TV beside the district attorney's large dark oak desk, Chief Gutierrez, from his own office, shared a split screen with US

Attorney Iris Chang and the attorney general. Behind Gutierrez, Cooper recognized the football trophy he proudly displayed that his oldest son had earned. A small reassuring memento in the dark news coming from the TV.

"The main thing," said the stiff-backed attorney general, "that we all want to emphasize is that there is *no cause* for undue alarm or concern. The resources of both the state of California and the federal government are fully mobilized in this investigation. All of us should go about our normal daily business, do what you need to do, and let the investigation move forward at the rapid pace we have established."

Walker grunted and said, "Gutierrez looks very unhappy."

"It comes with being stuck in no-man's land."

Guteirrez's role in the public play had been to outline in very broad terms the information known about the shooting. He blinked rapidly when Chang said firmly, "Let me echo what the attorney general and Chief Gutierrez said about letting normal life go on. We're all working very hard together to get answers and bring the responsible people to justice. And we're all agreed that no terrorist attack, no matter how cowardly, will deter our pursuit of justice for the perpetrators of these killings."

Cooper let his anger out. "Agent Walker, whatever you're telling your people isn't working. Ms. Chang's just given a road map for private reprisals. We're going to have people attacked because they're supposed to be terrorists."

"So get the answers, Cooper!" Walker flared. "Okay? If this isn't an assassination, get the goddamn answers and we'll shut this down before it gets worse."

"You're not cooperating," Cooper shot back angrily. "You know Booker was on the take. Get the AG to make a statement about it. At least throw cold water on the calls for vengeance." He had been shocked at the rapidity of some radio and editorial speculation about the foreign political motives for Booker's murder. There were already half-veiled warnings about boycotts, rough justice, and revenge. It had happened in less than a day.

"The only way to stop what's happening," Walker snapped, "is to wrap this up today, Cooper. I'll be on my cell. I've got to go get my agents," and he left.

Cooper looked at the TV again. Chief Gutierrez was about to say something, mouth opening, hunching forward, when his side of the screen went blank, leaving only Chang and the attorney general.

Must have lost the satellite link, Cooper thought coldly. *Couldn't* be anything else. Save the paranoia for later.

He sat down at Joyce Gutherie's desk and dialed her number in Florida.

"How are things holding up?" he asked when she answered.

"Unchanged," she said. "Thanks for asking, Dennis. I assume topic one in Sacramento is the same as topic one here?"

"Did you see the press conference?"

"Unfortunately, I did. Intentional or unintentional, it's going to make our job harder."

"Joyce . . . " He paused, wondering how to tell her. "Jerry Booker wasn't the victim of an assassination or a terrorist hit. That's becoming clearer everywhere we look."

"I think that's good news. But you don't sound like it is."

"There's no other way to tell you. Booker was taking bribes from companies coming before him in Congress. The FBI knows about it and they're not sharing much, but that much is plain fact. I've got Nye and Tafoya running down a witness the bureau generously provided unofficially." He took a breath. "I'm sorry. It's never good news when friends turn out to be less than we believed."

"No," she said quietly. "Do the bribes figure in what happened yesterday?"

"I think so. At least it's more likely than what we just heard at the press conference."

"So it will all be public sooner or later."

Cooper heard the flat resignation in her voice. "Probably."

"Well, when it does I'll either look very stupid as the DA who didn't know her friend and ally was corrupt, or maybe they'll say I was part of it somehow."

"Nobody's going to say that, Joyce. We're not responsible for our friends," *or perhaps in a fundamental way even those we love.* He knew it was hollow and false when he said it, though. She was right. The news of Booker's corruption, when it came out, would devastate her politically.

"I guess I can't worry about that now," she said. "Take care, Dennis. Thanks for your good thoughts."

"You take care, Joyce. I'll do everything I can."

He hung up. He thought of Sandy Drucker's sad commentary on people, the bribes offered inevitably, and he knew he had been offered his and taken it in the name of friendship and loyalty. His pledge to the DA to protect her as much as possible could be taken as trying to ensure that he kept his own job.

Macy, one of his newer deputies in Major Crimes, like Leah, stuck his head in the door. "Hey, Denny, Roseville cops got a mope tied to the .38. The guy's sitting across the street in our county jail. The damn gun angle just opened wide." He was grinning.

"I'm right behind you," he said, glad to be in action.

A very thin, sixty-eight-year-old Japanese-American cabdriver, according to his posted hack license, took Nye and Rose to Hancock Park, one of the older and very exclusive neighborhoods in Los Angeles. The lawns were verdant, the homes stately, the streets bounded by stone gates and wrought-iron fences. Nye leaned to Rose. "Give me the odds we get the only Japanese-American cabbie in the city and he's pushing retirement."

"Same odds as Lorenz picking Booker up. It's somebody's idea of a joke. And he drives carefully, Ter." Rose watched the very busy downtown Los Angeles streets they passed melt into each other, going from businesses and billboards advertising in Korean to Japanese to Spanish almost within blocks. The taxi turned north toward Hancock Park.

It took them thirty minutes to navigate the congested streets. The Los Angeles Police Department was everywhere, cops, cars, barricades. The residential neighborhood reminded Rose of Booker's home, the unreality of normally quiet and open spaces suddenly filled with tense and expectant armed strangers.

The Japanese Consulate occupied an early twentieth-century mansion on a corner. The endless police checks of bakery trucks and caterers, the search of the plainclothes private security guards brought in for the occasion, complicated the preparations for the birthday celebration. Rose asked their cabbie to wait.

They walked up the beautifully trimmed lawn. Nye said, "I know how the pukes feel. Everybody's watching us."

"No," she corrected. "Everybody's watching you. You stand out."

He inwardly acknowledged this was probably so. Rose looked cool and professional. He looked irritated and tired. The consulate's protocol official, a fussy and harried young woman in a traditional kimono, brought them into a small elegant room. It had a pleasant trace of roses. From its French windows, Nye saw musicians in tuxedoes and chefs darting around each other on the broad concrete apron of a large blue-watered pool.

A middle-aged Asian woman, dressed in light beige and bits of gold jewelry, greeted them. "I'm Mrs. Okura," she said, putting out a slim hand. "I don't quite understand why it was so urgent for you to see me and we're very, very occupied this morning."

Nye and Rose showed her their identification and introduced themselves. They had talked about how to handle this unusual witness on the flight down to LA. It was, Rose said, a little like playing twenty questions or hunting for evidence when they didn't really have a good idea what it might be. The one commonality in Booker's life, Rose suggested, was real estate: his new house, Manzoni's real estate materials in the district office. Don't forget the cars and the money, Terry added. Maybe that's the deal.

They all sat down. The musicians tuned up and swung into rehearsing a muted waltz.

"Mrs. Okura," Rose began, "we appreciate your time today. We need to ask you some questions about Congressman Gerald Booker."

"How terrifying," she said a little nervously. "The police wanted us to cancel the celebration because of security concerns. But this birthday reception is an annual highlight of the city's calendar. This afternoon we will have most of the city council, members of Congress and the legislature, representatives from eighteen nations here to drink to the emperor's health. We can't cancel it. The consul was adamant. All precautions will be taken, but paying respect to the emperor today must go on."

"Did you know Congressman Booker?"

"I never met him. I don't know anything about him."

Rose glanced at Nye.

Mrs. Okura continued brusquely. "I must get back to the preparations. The chef from the New Otani Hotel is bringing a special sushi appetizer and I've got to show him where he can finish it. The only contact I had with Representative Booker was to make a twenty-thousand-dollar contribution to his next campaign."

Rose didn't have to feign confusion. "Why did you contribute so much to his campaign if you don't know anything about him?"

Nye waited with great curiosity. This sounded like the setup to a gag.

But Mrs. Okura was straight-faced and impatient. "I have an insurance business and I'm very active in many civic organizations in Japantown, Koreatown, and Chinatown. I was offered a very attractive opportunity to buy a new home not far from here."

"Who offered?" Nye asked.

"An old friend, the president of a Korean language media firm. I bought the home at a quite reasonable price—" and Nye interrupted.

"How reasonable? Below market?"

"I drive a very hard bargain. I'm a very persuasive business-woman," she said with more than a touch of pride. "I made a deal to buy the house for almost sixty thousand less than it was originally on the market for."

"Didn't that much of a drop strike you as unusual?"

"Well, as I said, I negotiated vigorously. I was told the owner was leaving California suddenly and needed to sell quickly."

Nye cocked his head. "How does this involve Booker?"

"Just about the time we were finishing the details so I could buy the house, I got a call from my friend at the Korean firm. He said I should talk to a man named Ralph Payton before we signed the escrow on the house. I called him."

Rose gave nothing away. She could have been going through the routine of filling out a library card application. "Who was Mr. Payton?"

"He knew many of the people I worked with, so I was surprised I'd never met him," and for the first time a hint of uneasiness and defiance entered her voice. "We shared the same interest in helping our communities and he said that Congressman Booker was trying to accomplish the same things we were, better schools, city services, encouraging investment."

"You write big checks because someone tells you a guy's a prince over the phone?" Nye was deliberately sharp to see what she did.

Mrs. Okura blushed instantly. "Mr. Payton was referred by a man I knew well and worked with. People in our communities buy shares in companies with their whole life savings because friends or people in their church do it too. It's a bond built on trust."

"How did this bond express itself?" Rose asked politely, demonstrating that she disapproved of Nye's rudeness. Mrs. Okura took the bait.

"Mr. Payton described a way I could help Congressman Booker and my community by making a contribution to his campaign committee. He gave me the amount that was required and I wrote a check that afternoon." She waited. "I did nothing wrong. I reported my contribution within ten days. You can look it up yourself."

Rose nodded so that Nye would appear to be on a leash. Nye sniffed the perfumed air and pretended to listen to the new waltz outside and the cries for more grills.

"Mrs. Okura, did you think the house deal would fall apart if you didn't make this contribution?"

"I had no reason to think that," she said defensively. "But I also saw no reason to be ungrateful for the opportunity I had been given."

"Did Mr. Payton get in touch with you for any more contributions?"

"No, it was only that one. I did"—she licked her thin lips—"suggest other businesspeople he might contact, people who would appreciate the chance to buy a home for themselves or as an investment."

Nye stood up. "You got to get back to your sushi and we're on a plane. Thanks for seeing us," and he gave her his card.

Mrs. Okura escorted them to the mansion's front door. More caterers were arriving and being inspected by the police. "I described these events exactly the same way to the FBI six months ago. Is the congressman's death somehow connected to anything I told them or you?"

"We're investigating a lot of possibilities," Rose said diplomatically. "You've been very helpful."

"Just as long as it's clear I simply bought a home. People do that every day." She closed the door.

Nye and Rose walked back to their taxi. "I got one word for you," he said to her. "Kickback."

"She knows it. Payton maybe didn't lay it out like that, but I bet he made her understand the terms. No contribution, no house. She runs the numbers and she's still forty thousand ahead."

"Nice gag," Nye admitted. "Laundering the payoff through a real estate sale turns it into a contribution from a big donor. Big donor's contribution is reported, looks clean as a whistle. This lady points Payton to other marks in the community he can hit."

Rose climbed into the front seat of the taxi. "I bet we find that the Korean company's one of Payton's clients. The whole thing's a big shell game."

"Cooper's going to love it. You got the cone of silence over this deal, people talking to pals who set them up with great real estate bargains, kickback cash, and no one talks because everyone's happy."

Rose nodded. "We're going back to the airport," she told the old cabbie.

He put the taxi in gear. He had been gazing at the flurry of activity at the consulate. "Wait until my mom hears about this tonight," he said. "She and my dad would've loved coming to this."

Leah left the coffee the sergeant brought her on a steel shelf identical to the seemingly endless rows of steel shelving that stretched in all directions around her. She wasn't sure where it was now. Packed from the floor to just over her head on the shelves were decades of crimes and misdemeanors committed in the city of Sacramento. It was in its perverse way a history of the city and its people, perhaps a more accurate history than the battles over power and money in the capitol.

Felony files were red-tagged. Misdemeanor files were blue-tagged. She traced the years and the names, bending down when the files were on low shelves. Fat, thin, ragged with pages, neat and contained, the files were stupefying in their numbers.

Leah coughed a little at the dust. Sacramento was still surrounded by a large number of fields and farms. The dust was part of that agricultural productivity. It was fine and ubiquitous. It lightly dusted the old case files and she stirred it up when she walked along the concrete aisles or pulled files out.

She checked her printout several times. Twenty years ago, Booker had some contact with law enforcement in Sacramento. Judge Roche had represented him on a drunk driving case or some crime involving drunk driving. So Leah was disappointed when she found a Booker blue-tagged file in the right year. It was a four-fifteen, a disturbing-the-peace offense. She read the file quickly because it was short, as she leaned against the steel shelves.

Gerald Booker, stationed at McClellan Air Force Base, had gotten into a fight at the Ram Bar in north Sacramento just before Labor Day. He was cut when his head hit a table and the wound required stitches. So much for the old war injury, she thought. He never claimed he got it during the Gulf War. He just let people draw the wrong conclusion. The other two men involved were uninjured. Leah flipped the flimsy pages. Booker paid a fine and got three years of informal probation that expired without incident. The public defender was Roche, which explained her representing him on the other case. Public defenders were often assigned to the same defendant when new cases came in, especially when they were close in time.

She pushed the file back into its place on the shelf. A minor disturbing-the-peace case didn't match the strange entry on Booker's printout. There had to be another case. Roche had represented him on another case. Leah frowned. Maybe Denny was right. This was a waste of time.

She spent the next hour trying to find any other files with Booker's name on them. There were nearly a dozen Bookers who committed various crimes from bank robbery to forgery, but only the lone Gerald Booker case.

It was getting late in the morning and she had witness statements to work on and telephone records to review back at her office. With any luck, the Roseville and Santa Rosa police had found something about the gun.

She decided she should find where she had left the coffee instead of letting the sergeant stumble on it someday. It would be discourteous after he had been helpful.

She prowled around the stacks futilely for ten minutes, growing annoyed as she turned each identical corner and found herself apparently back in the same place, although it was in fact a different stack of steel shelves.

Leah was thoughtful. One thing was obvious. If a simple disturbing-the-peace case file had survived twenty years, then a drunk-driving case should have as well. Unless it was misplaced, which could have happened any time during those decades, or someone had deliberately removed it entirely. She stopped.

Pulling a criminal file was itself a crime. No one commits one crime to conceal another unless the crime being hidden is more damaging or dangerous.

And the only people who had access to these files, here or when they were still at SPD, were law enforcement personnel, cops or DAs.

She walked on slowly. Ahead on a shelf, she found her coffee, stone cold. This was the row of files she had started checking and found nothing with Booker's name on it. She looked again, more slowly, prying the tightly packed files apart.

Which was where she found it, a slim file, probably only a single page, red-tagged. Easily overlooked by her. Or anyone else hunting for a bulky case file with reports and other documents in it.

GERALD F. BOOKER, it said in black marking pen on the buff-colored folder. She opened it. Two pages, photocopies, now brittle, of summary pages of another case. A duplicate cover document that had gotten stuck into a separate file. But there was enough to see what the other case had been. Leah was a little surprised that her enthusiasm to track down the file was undimmed once she found this vestige of it. She read as she started walking quickly. Denny needed to see this.

Judge Roche had been accurate when she bitterly referred to defending Booker. It was a defense against a drunk driving charge, but it had started out as something worse, and that must have burned in her over the years when she could say nothing because Jerry Booker had been her client.

My God, Leah thought, it's been a nightmare for him and everybody else. Trapped and he couldn't escape. She had seen a familiar name in the brittle photocopy. It all started here, she realized, and it ended yesterday.

The sergeant smiled broadly. "Find what you wanted?"

Leah signed for the file. She dug out her cell phone to call Cooper. "Maybe everything." She turned briefly. "That was a great cup of coffee."

"Okay. The wife says she could use it to kill weeds."

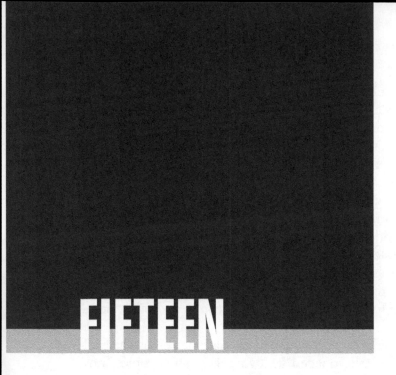

FIFTEEN

TWO MEN SAT ACROSS FROM Cooper in an interview room at the Sacramento County Jail. One had on a baggy gray suit with two small cigarette holes burned on the trousers. He had rumpled salt-and-pepper hair and yellow teeth and he looked seasick.

The other man was handcuffed to the metal table in the room. He sat opposite a two-way mirror. He was black, young, and his shaven head was so ovoid and his neck so skinny he reminded Cooper of a lamp without a shade.

"Mr. Kincaid," Cooper said to the seasick man, "I'm not interested in your client's receiving-stolen-property case. I don't care where he got the plasma TVs." His cell phone went off but he didn't answer it.

"I want a deal," the young man burst out. "I paid a fucking lot of money for those TVs." He cursed rhythmically and inventively.

"I think Mr. Lebaron should get a deal, Cooper, if you want to talk to him about some gun he doesn't own—" and Cooper broke in.

"At this moment, I can link your client to a Smith and Wesson .38 that was used in two armed robberies in this area in the last few years."

"I will bet you can't or you would've done it instead of looking at his brother Jerome," Kincaid said, belched, and excused himself. *"This* Mr. Lebaron is entitled to consideration on his current matter if you want to ask him," and belched again. He swallowed. "I need a smoke."

Cooper got up. Lebaron stared ahead at the mirror, either admiring his reflection or trying to pierce behind it to see who might be watching him. They were alone, though. Cooper hadn't even told Walker yet. He thought that it would be more productive to talk to Lebaron without the lurking threat of the FBI close at hand.

"Mr. Lebaron, let's understand your situation. You're facing prison on three counts of felony receiving stolen property because of 110 plasma TVs taken from Circuit City found in your home a week ago. You have a prior receiving conviction. Your option today is to do that time or do it with an additional ten years added on for the two armed robberies."

"I want a deal. I. Want. A. Deal," he repeated and he cursed at his attorney.

"Steven," Kincaid said, "Steven. Let me handle this. Your family hired me to help you."

Cooper waited for the drama of dealing with a difficult client to conclude. He didn't want either Lebaron or his under-the-weather lawyer to know how much he needed to trace the .38 from Lebaron onward. Nor had he told either of them that the .38 was the one that had killed Booker and Lorenz. While the gravity of the crimes might stimulate Lebaron to talk, Cooper had seen it close doors instantly. He couldn't risk it.

"What's it going to be, Mr. Lebaron? Doing time for receiving a la carte or as part of a full menu?"

"How about this, Cooper?" Kincaid said soothingly, belching once. "You won't charge *this* Mr. Lebaron for either of the offenses you mentioned and you'll give him a pass on anything else that might come up involving this gun. *Assuming* he knows anything about it."

Cooper pretended to weigh the offer. "It's a deal as long as I get the truth and I can trace the weapon, but I'm not dealing away crimes I don't know about."

Steven Lebaron raised his eyebrows. "What the fuck kind of deal's that?"

"It's the best you're going to get, Mr. Lebaron. It expires in one minute."

"This is a good offer, Steven. Trust me." Kincaid covered his mouth.

Cooper waited anxiously in the pause. He knew he had succeeded when Lebaron dropped his eyes from the mirror, no longer entranced by his own defiant image. "All right," he said disgustedly, "go ahead. I'll tell you about the fucking Russian."

Cooper brought out a yellow legal pad and a green felt-tip pen. A Russian? Nothing in the investigation had turned up any Russian. Before he could ask Lebaron a question, Kincaid stood up, belching repeatedly.

"I may need a *teeny* break," he said. "A not entirely satisfied client paid me with homemade garlic sausage and I don't think it's *agreeing* with me."

Twenty minutes later, Kincaid had returned shaken from the men's room. Cooper in the meantime had spoken to Leah about what she found in the records, the old records that held old sins in them like flies trapped forever in amber. Booker had a particularly unpleasant old sin chalked up against him and more, someone else who had known about it for a very long time. Leah said, "It looks like blackmail, Denny. Pure and simple. June was his alibi. She used it to get anything she wanted from him."

"If it is blackmail, it's gone on so long Booker may have forgotten about it. It was just part of how his life ended up."

"Oh no," Leah said emphatically, "I don't think he forgot for one day all these years. I think it explains why he was making a break with that speech. He was blowing it all up. He was leaving her."

"So it's a motive to kill him. The blackmailer was enraged."

"I'm going to look at the telephone records again for the last couple of days and see how this plays into who he was talking to. We need to go out and reinterview June Booker right away."

"Great. I'm going to get some critical material from Mr. Lebaron as soon as his lawyer stops throwing up. Walker's people can run down the .38. I want to go over the old file summary with Nye and Tafoya. Maybe they dig up some details when they hit the widow Booker again." He chuckled. "Good work, Deputy Fisher. Your long shot may give us a big boost."

"When was the .38 Smith and Wesson last in your possession, Mr. Lebaron?" Cooper asked. Steven Lebaron had diet Dr Pepper in a paper cup and he gulped half of it. His attorney rocked slowly in the chair beside him, still looking seasick.

"Okay, here it is. I got this gun from someone—" and Cooper broke in.

"I don't care where you got it. When did you have it last?"

"About six, seven, maybe eight months ago. See, I needed to get rid of it, old revolver, kind of an antique, right? Looks bad, like your auntie's gun. Besides, I needed to get my nine, like everybody."

Cooper knew he meant a 9mm Glock, the weapon of choice in the majority of shootings he encountered. The .38 S&W had a quaintness about it that made it distinctive and therefore also a liability for anyone using it in a crime. It could be easily connected to one person. It had reliability, though, and a virtue Steven Lebaron might not have appreciated: Because it was a revolver it discharged no shell casings when it was fired. The Glock, as an automatic, left identifiable shell casings at the crime scene.

"Did you trade the .38 for a Glock?"

"Nah, I gave it away. I got fifty bucks for it. I got my nine couple days before, so I didn't need it."

Kincaid smiled vaguely. He was probably deciding to get his fees in other forms than homemade edibles that could, through clumsiness or calculation, be poisonous.

"Who did you sell the .38 to?"

Lebaron blew out a long breath. "Okay, see, I know this guy at Raley's Market on Freeport. I mean, I don't *know* him, but I see him bringing boxes in and out, he works their loading dock, I pass by on my own business, and we got to talking one day."

"Who is this guy?"

"Okay, see, he's like Russian. From Russia, right? Lot of them in town now, I see them all over, they got car repair shops, restaurants, I do some business with them sometimes."

Kincaid rolled his eyes. "I don't think we need to get into any of this, Steven."

Cooper had been writing, nodding, every gesture unthreatening and deliberate. Witnesses or suspects talked candidly because they felt, no matter if they were frightened or angry to start with, unthreatened at that moment. "What's his name, the Russian?"

"Okay, so one morning, I'm going by, he's having a smoke, he's all mad and he's saying shit in Russian. So I get into it with him for a little bit, turns out he's pissed off because the store's got him working graveyard, nobody helping, he's really tired, and they just got him down for more shifts and no more money. You know."

Still no name, Cooper thought.

"So, he asks me, can I get him a gun? I say, why? He says, he got to have a gun to take care of himself because everybody's disrespecting him." Lebaron finished the Dr Pepper. "He's mad, man. Really, really mad. I could see him doing serious harm."

"You sold him the .38?"

"Next day, maybe eight that night, we go together at this little club on Broadway, did the deal in the parking lot. He's got the gun, I got fifty, everybody's taken care of."

Cooper put the green pen down. "Did he make any specific threats? Name any people?"

"His lady, she's another Russian. She's seeing some guy from Minsky or Pinsky or something, and he's going crazy." Lebaron ticked off his fingers. "He had it down for the managers at the store, the drivers who gave him shit when he unloaded their trucks, he had a *real* long list, man." Lebaron laughed and squeezed his sides.

But no Congressman Gerald Booker apparently.

Kincaid groaned. "All I'm saying, Cooper, is that you made the deal."

"And I intend to honor it," Cooper said, sliding his chair back, standing up, and staring hard at Steven Lebaron, "as soon as your client gives me the name and address of the man he sold the .38 to."

"Please, Steven. Fun and games later."

"Okay, yeah." Lebaron stopped laughing. "His name is Mike Kokoshkin."

"A Russian named Mike?"

"No, like *Mikhail.* He showed me his immigration card one time."

"Address?"

"Hell I know that? Raley's on Freeport, man. Ask them."

Cooper had gotten off the phone with Rose Tafoya when Leah got back. Rose told him about Mrs. Okura and the scheme that turned kickbacks into unblemished campaign contributions. "I've got a chore for you and Nye," he said. "Something's come up about June Booker."

"Terry and I'll come to your office as soon as we land," Rose said.

Leah was excitedly showed him the slim summary file. "I guess what happened is that Booker got the original charge dumped down because June alibied him, so he pleaded out to a misdemeanor, got it expunged a couple of years later."

Cooper shook his head. "The file should've still been there, Leah. Even if a court took it off his record."

"I know. Sometime in the last ten, fifteen years, the original case file was taken out of records. Booker was probably running for Congress, or maybe he was running for reelection. Someone didn't want it found."

Cooper read the flimsy pages again and let out a breath. "Another bribe. A clerk or a cop makes a file disappear."

Leah sat down. There was, she thought, a strange almost holiday expectancy hanging over the office and the city, perhaps even the country. It was as if everyone was waiting. But she didn't think everyone waited for something fun or enjoyable. The brightness and lightness just before a weekend or a holiday were everywhere as she saw people on the streets or in the building. It was, though, the expectancy of going on a vacation from routine, rules, laws.

We're all looking for an excuse to go wild, she thought. She felt it herself.

Kids without parents. Nobody who could say *don't*. This is wrong. This is evil.

"Leah?" Cooper asked. "You usually don't look spooked."

"I am today."

He checked the clock above his overcrowded bookcase. Denny interposed activity between his own fear and uncertainty. He imposed structure. "Nye and Tafoya should be back in about an hour. Let's run June Booker, Manzoni, and Payton through their paces with what you brought back and what Terry and Rose got about the kickbacks to Booker."

"You've got SPD working on the Russian?"

"Drier and his team are checking Kokoshkin's last employer. I have no idea how he fits in, but he's the best lead to Booker's actual shooting. Maybe this is dangerous." He grinned coolly. "But for the first time since this landed on all of us, I feel a little optimistic we're going to close it out today."

"I hope so," Leah said. Cooper had two small TVs on a table near the window. Leah pointed at the soundless images, a straggly line of people snaking into the state capitol under the vigilant gaze of dozens of armed troops, the endlessly repeated clip of June Booker in black being escorted, stiffly staring ahead, into the white stone building to view her husband's casket. On the other TV, angry immigrants in Lodi and Stockton gathering to protest the FBI's mass interviews. "Everybody's waiting for a sign, Denny. Then all hell's going to break loose."

"Agent Walker's very pleased with the number of immigration violations they've turned up in the last five hours. It appears productive," and Cooper laid sarcastic emphasis on the last word.

The phone on his desk loudly buzzed. He scanned the caller ID and punched the speaker. "Agent Walker. Ms. Fisher and I were just discussing you."

Walker's voice was tight and angry. "When did you see Sandy Drucker, Cooper?"

"Early this morning. I told you that. About two."

Silence. Heavy, furious, and implacable. Leah looked questioningly at Cooper.

Then Walker said, "I'm going to give you an address in West Sacramento. Why don't you and Fisher come on out and meet me?"

"What's going on?" Cooper snapped.

"Drucker's dead. Somebody did a job on her. Goddamn, Cooper, you let her walk away last night."

"We'll be right there," he said, feeling stunned, jotting down the address Walker spat out.

Leah slowly turned off the TVs and their provocatively colliding pictures washing incessantly over the state and the country.

SIXTEEN

THE TWO-STORY SQUAT MOTEL in West Sacramento was off Harbor Boulevard, nestled in seedy garishness among heavy equipment yards, the flashing neons against the blue morning of liquor and adult bookstores, not far from the Port of Sacramento.

Walker met them in the parking lot crowded with police cars from both cities. TV cameras were being set up on the sidewalk, and the crowd, drawn magnetically by the activity, had started to gather.

"This is the first stop," he said tersely. "We'll get to the main attraction next."

"I thought she was here," Cooper said.

Leah spoke briefly to one of the half-dozen FBI agents moving in and out of the room on the second floor.

"She's not here. There's an old friend you should see before we get to Drucker. It's a comedy, Cooper. I swear to God, it is." There was no trace of amusement in his voice.

Leah bent to Cooper as they strode up the outside stairs to the rooms on the second floor. "One of Walker's guys told me they're working this with you to take the fall, Denny. We've got to be careful."

"I'd probably do the same to them," he said dispassionately, trying to suppress his wrenching guilt.

Room 232 was uncomfortably busy. It had a twin bed, stripped to the rumpled sheets, faded ceramic lamps, and a battered TV bolted to the wall. At a cracked table, in his boxer briefs, Deputy Chief Layne sat glumly. His pale legs and sagging white chest were speckled with gray hair. He stared at his reflection in the wall mirror, watching the people behind him as if they were on TV.

Cooper noted Leah taking in everything. On the edge of the bed sat two naked enormously obese black women, wrapped in parts of sheets. They were loudly arguing with two West Sacramento cops and an FBI agent.

"Shut up!" Walker shouted at the women, who gaped at him momentarily, then resumed their high-decibel protests. "Get them out, get them out." He swept his arms forward, and the two women were hauled up awkwardly, looking grandly like Romans in togas, and marched outside, their voices even louder because they were upset that people would laugh at them.

"Miles?" Cooper said quietly. Walker stood beside Leah. The cops were bagging items on a cigarette-burn-scored bedside table.

"Hello, Dennis," the deputy chief said. "Hello, Leah." He sounded very tired.

Walker turned to Leah, as though the deputy chief was deaf. "This one's been with two hookers, the charmers who just left, since around midnight. Right there"—he pointed at the bedside table—"we've got a little bit of coke, a little bit of meth, a little bit of weed. Nice buffet for a fun-filled night."

Cooper's guilt about Sandy Drucker's murder was now mixed with an overpowering sensation of shame for Deputy Chief Layne. They were not friends but they saw each other frequently officially and at the many parties, lunches, and dinners that bound the area's law enforcement community together. They were members of the same tribe, and now Cooper realized he didn't recognize this shrunken, gray and white old man sitting in front of the fly-specked mirror.

"We should thank this one," Walker went on savagely. "Because if he hadn't decided to relax last night, we probably wouldn't have found Drucker. What happened, Cooper and Fisher, is pretty funny, if you look at it a certain way. This one's got his hookers, his dope, and he's got their pimp. The pimp's on searchable parole. The pimp goes out around five this morning to get some more . . . " He stared at Layne. "What was it? Meth? You all finished off the meth and you needed a refill?"

"This isn't necessary," Leah said firmly.

"You bet it is," Walker barked. "So the pimp goes to *his* pal at a roach motel even worse than this. That's when the pimp, because he's loaded, crashes into a Dumpster, knocks it over, and out falls what's left of our witness Sandy Drucker. Local cops are cruising by, they grab the pimp, they run him, they find Drucker, they find out he's on searchable and in his pants pocket"—Walker held up a maroon-tagged key—"he's got this room key and he gives up the deputy chief here and his ladies in a fast heartbeat. He needs a really good alibi, right? You can't get a better alibi than a deputy chief of the Sacramento Police Department."

"Miles." Cooper came to the table. He wished there was something to cover Layne with. "What are you doing here?"

Walker started to answer, and Cooper cut him off with a glare.

The deputy chief shifted on the chair, hands clasped forward, as if praying. "I finished after midnight, and the chief tells me he's getting heat and it's over. I figured I could make it for another year or two, kind of make the retirement work better. I needed that. But the chief"—he shook his head bitterly—"he said he had to show he was in charge of a tight department with all this publicity and now was my time. Two weeks he gave me."

"I'm sorry, Miles."

"I couldn't go home. My wife's been sick for a while, you know. I made a call." He sat back wearily. "It's not the first time."

Walker laughed harshly. "Hell no. He's a goddamn regular. He likes to watch those two charmers go at it."

Leah said, "I think we're done here. We should go to the other crime scene."

Layne winced slightly as she spoke. "Dennis, is there anything you can help me with here?"

Cooper saw Walker's wolfish anticipation. He'd pounce on any sign of sympathy for Layne. But the truth was that Cooper didn't feel anything except bewilderment and sadness. He was reminded once again that no one knows another human being, not to the core, and maybe even a lot less than that. Leah had a stony expression. She had drawn a line long ago, and people like Miles Layne were on the other side from her.

"No, Miles. I can't do anything," Cooper said.

A long, slow sigh, like air leaking from a balloon, came from Layne. "I wish I had my piece," he said calmly.

Cooper swung to Walker. "All right, the show's over. I want to see Drucker."

The second crime scene was behind the Plantation Motel two miles away, a decaying cinder block box that looked like a bunker. The area was yellow-taped to close it off. Techs and two crime scene vans were working in the alley. Walker led them forward. A large battered green Dumpster was tipped onto its side, a flood of garbage spilled over the asphalt. In the middle of the colorful and stinking mass lay Sandy Drucker, wearing only a blue skirt and one shoe. As Cooper and Leah approached, she seemed to be watching them, her glass-hard dead eyes fixed in their direction.

The slender county medical examiner, Dr. Fabiani, stepped gingerly across the garbage. He had been studying the body.

"Cooper and Ms. Fisher," he said brightly. "They tell me the victim is connected to your dead congressman."

"Mistress," Leah said tightly.

"Killing one politician gives people ideas," the ME said mockingly. "Like eating potato chips."

"Tell them what you know right now," Walker said.

"Certainly. The victim is about forty, white female. Shot four times at close range in the head. Death was instantaneous."

Cooper's feeling of remorse was overwhelming. *I should've had her arrested last night. Talked her out of leaving. Something. Something!*

As though it was possible to change much of anything.

Leah spoke a little shakily. "I can see the head wounds, Doctor. What are those marks on her shoulders and breasts?"

Walker grunted. He wanted Cooper to hear this horror.

"Well, burns of some kind. From the irregular shape, I'd say they're from an old car cigarette lighter. The whorled pattern is fairly distinctive."

"She was tortured," Cooper said. "Somebody wanted information about, what? What did she know?"

Walker bent to the body, examining the otherwise unremarkable four blood-black entry wounds to the head. "Tell me, Cooper. You let her go."

Leah answered, walking around to view the body from the side, "She was Booker's mistress and whoever killed him thought she knew something very important. Torturing her must have taken a while."

"She was tied. There are ligature marks on her ankles and wrists and she struggled." The techs were snapping photos as Fabiani talked. "I'll leave it to the FBI and SPD to determine where she was killed. Although if it was here"—he looked up at the Plantation Motel—"I suspect loud noises are fairly common."

"One problem," Walker said, straightening up and pointing at Drucker's body, "with linking her to Booker's shooting. She was killed with a .22, no exit wounds."

"Booker and Lorenz were shot with a .38 and we're trying to locate the last known owner," Cooper said, reciting the well-known facts to block how he felt. He could see people in neighboring buildings looking down at the wreckage in the alley from their windows or balconies. In every mind, regardless of who or why they came to stare, ran the same relieved thought: *At least it isn't me.*

Leah came back to Walker, Cooper, and Fabiani. "It works out like this. Dennis leaves Drucker around two. She's in her own car. We need to find her car. Sometime after that, she either meets accidentally or contacts or is contacted by a person who persuades her to come with him."

"Or she was forced," Walker said.

"She was very frightened when I saw her," Cooper said. "She was going into hiding. I can't imagine her seeking anybody out, and anybody who could talk her into going with them would have to be very good." He couldn't get her panicked, shocked voice out of his mind.

"Maybe," Leah conceded. "In any case, she's tortured for some time to find out something and then dumped here under the garbage."

"I would add," Fabiani said smugly, "you should look for someone with a .22 who also owns an older model vehicle. Cigarette lighters haven't been standard equipment for years now."

"Agent Walker, you should deploy some of your people to work with SPD on locating Drucker's car. Dr. Fabiani will retrieve the .22 slugs and we can run those for identification with a weapon. You can spare a few agents from their immigration interviews," Cooper said with uncharacteristic rancor.

Leah and Fabiani were startled by what Walker did next. Cooper seemed to have expected it. Walker leaned forward, a fist cocked and with an effort of willpower, he pulled back. Cooper was unflinching.

"Listen," Walker rasped, "I am officially ending the joint investigation, you sorry, pathetic screwup. This is from the Department of Justice, direct to your chief of police, stay out of my way. If you, Cooper, or you, Fisher, get in the way of me or my agents, I will arrest both of you and I won't even think about it."

The cops, techs, and FBI agents all stopped where they were, uncertain how to react to Walker's and Cooper's bitter quarrel.

"The ME can stay," Walker went on, rapid-fire, "because he's started the postmortem protocol. But every other nonfederal asshole is to clear out from my crime scene," he shouted, "and I mean *now!*"

He snapped gestures at the FBI agents, who began moving cops and techs they had been working with a few minutes before, away and toward the yellow tape. Fabiani seemed bemused by the infighting and stepped into the garbage again and carefully knelt beside the body.

The abruptness of what had happened caught Leah off-guard. Cooper had already made his decision, driven to it by Drucker's murder and his own mistakes. "All right. Everybody from SPD and the West Sac department, please pack it up."

"Denny?" Leah asked angrily.

"We choose our battles," he said to her quietly. "We'll go win our own war." To Walker he snapped, "Agent Walker, the warning goes for your people too. I won't hesitate to arrest anyone who interferes in our investigation."

Walker turned away and Cooper decided to play a hunch that had been growing in conviction for the last few hours.

Cooper called out to Walker, "Drucker was working for you, wasn't she? She was your informant."

"Are you nuts?" Walker said, stalking back to him. "Have you completely lost your fucking mind, Cooper?"

Calmly, his steely rage controlled, Cooper said, "You've been hiding material information from me from the beginning about Booker. You've been working on him for a while obviously. You've recruited a white-collar team to put together a case against him, kickbacks and bribes, misuse of office. Our cops confirmed today the only lead you gave us, the money-laundering scheme. I'm betting you got enough for Washington to green-light a full-scale investigation. In a corruption investigation, that means electronic surveillance and snitches, Agent Walker. We thought of going after Payton but we never had anyone who'd wear a wire, who'd be our informant. You got Sandy Drucker to be your snitch and you've got everything Booker told her on tape."

Walker shook his head, muttering.

Leah folded her arms, thinking. It made terrible sense. It had terrible logic and the conclusion was inescapable.

Cooper turned his anger on Walker suddenly. "Because Sandy Drucker was your snitch, you had an obligation to protect her. You owed her that. She was brutally murdered because you failed, Agent Walker. Someone had to find out if she was an informant. Someone killed her last night because she was working for you."

Leah touched his arm. "No, Denny, listen—" she started to say.

But Walker looked up, hands in his pockets, incredulity on his face. "That is all bullshit, Cooper. Drucker wasn't my snitch."

"You're lying," Cooper said flatly, with utter certainty.

Leah grabbed his arm. "Denny, wait a second," she said. But Cooper was silently, coldly exultant that he had exposed Walker's abject failure and duplicity. He didn't hear her. It helped a little to quench the pain that he had let Drucker down, too.

The inevitable TV camera trucks were showing up, like scavengers drawn by carrion. They screeched to a stop at the far end of the alley. Cooper had a brief image of an enterprising TV crew perching in one of the surrounding buildings, pointing their relentless cameras down on the victim and the fighting FBI agent and DA.

Walker spotted the TV cameras too, and he knew Fabiani and everyone nearby could hear him. He came close to Cooper, his voice venomous, low. "I've worked with some stupid sons of bitches, guys who didn't know their ass from a hole in the ground. But you are at the head of the parade, Cooper. You're the grand marshal. Drucker was *not* working for me, repeat, she was *not* my snitch at any time or any way. She loved that dishonest, crooked motherfucker and she wouldn't do a goddamn thing to hurt him."

Cooper listened, every insult confirming that he had scored a direct hit on the arrogant FBI special agent.

"Booker was my snitch," Walker spat.

Cooper didn't comprehend the words until he looked at Leah. She understood immediately. Walker kept talking.

"I had him wired up for a couple dozen meetings with congressional staffers and his buddies. I have them on video and audio, Cooper. I made a deal with Booker and then he went public because his fucking conscience started to bother him or he got impatient. Now that he's dead, I can't use the tapes in court. I can't authenticate them. He got himself killed and now I've got boxes of home movies of congressmen sticking marked government money in their pockets and I can't do a goddamn thing with them."

"It makes sense, Denny," Leah said. "Booker was killed because he was a snitch and someone knew about it. He probably told someone." She looked over at the body sprawled in the Dumpster's garbage. "Whoever killed Booker thought Sandy Drucker knew too. She was tortured to find out how much she knew."

Walker nodded. "Yeah. Now get the hell out of here." He went over to his agents.

Cooper didn't move for a moment. Then he strode quickly toward their car, Leah with him. "What the hell have I done?" he said with immense angry remorse. "Christ, Leah, what the hell else have I missed?"

"It's not only you," she said, but that didn't help.

SEVENTEEN

NYE AND ROSE WERE WAITING for them when Cooper and Leah got back to the office. Nye shrugged at Rose when she inquiringly noted Cooper's ragged, set features and his clipped words.

All around them phones rang in the office. There had been a skirmish with police and recent immigrants in St. Louis and it was everywhere on the news. Chief Gutierrez was moving his cops into potential trouble spots around the city. A fight had broken out in the line of people waiting to see Jerry Booker in the capitol rotunda. It was just a little after noon.

Cooper didn't sit down. He and Leah gave the two detectives a blunt summary of Walker's revelation and what was known about Drucker's brutal killing. Nye coarsely dismissed the special agent's ultimatum about staying clear of his investigation. "Fibbies didn't bring anything to the table anyway. They better stay away from us."

"I don't get the Russian," Rose said.

"Either someone hired him or the gun moved on. We'll

track it," Cooper said. "Right now, I want you both to locate Payton and Manzoni. Work both of them as hard as you can."

"Can we get a fanulu warrant if we can't fill in all the blanks?" Nye asked lightly. He was trying to leaven the gloomy atmosphere. He meant an arrest warrant in which either the first name was unknown, or FNU, or the last name was unknown, LNU. Judges despised reviewing warrants that lacked information, but sometimes speed and exigent circumstances made it unavoidable.

"This isn't a joke, Detective," Cooper said. "Leah's going to tell you what we know about Booker's rap sheet. She found an old vehicular homicide that's been buried for twenty years and June Booker has been using it for all that time."

"Jesus," Rose breathed.

"The old case may give us some direction. These people are all knotted together," Leah said. "Blackmail was part of bribes, and they're part of kickbacks."

"Okay, Chief," Nye said. "Payton and Manzoni are up next." He yawned. "I'm way past my bedtime."

"I'll smack him a little," Rose promised.

Cooper headed for the door. "I'm going to see June Booker. She was with Drucker two days ago and she's been lying to us. Leah, hold things down here and make sure Walker stays away from our people. Maybe you'd better tell the detectives about Deputy Chief Layne." He had deliberately left out that bleak detail.

"Thanks," she said without meaning it.

Leah took Rose and Nye back to her office. He kept looking at his watch and then drumming his fingers on his chair. "We need to get started," he said.

"I'll make it quick," Leah said, unfazed by cop impatience. Rose smirked at Nye's mood swing. Hearing about Miles Layne as they went to Leah's office had aroused his combative side. He had cursed long and colorfully, then lapsed into silence as the facts sank in. Now he wanted to get out, roam the city streets in search of their targets.

She gave Rose the brief summary file on Booker. Rose read it quickly and handed it to Nye. Leah rattled off what was in it, and what could be surmised.

Labor Day, twenty years earlier, sometime after eight P.M. a young man named Larry Johnson was walking home along a slough road just outside Sacramento, the sun fading. It was a lightly traveled road alongside a vast cornfield. A pickup truck driving at high speed struck Johnson, flinging him fifteen feet down the road and into the deep gully that ran beside the slough. The driver of the pickup apparently went on without stopping. Johnson's parents, concerned that he hadn't come home, called friends and finally the police, but there was no sign of him. Medical evidence later determined that he had a broken back, both legs shattered, and a fractured skull. He survived for twelve hours in the shallow water of the ditch until he died of his injuries. A young air force pilot, Gerald Booker, got up the next morning and told the girlfriend he was visiting that he thought he might have hit a deer the night before when he was driving to see her. He had brought her a load of furniture lashed in the bed of his pickup. His girlfriend took a look at the truck and discovered a large dent in the right front fender and the windshield on the passenger side smashed and bloodied. She advised Booker to retrace his route and see if there was an injured animal. He drove out slowly and was horrified to find the body of Larry Johnson in the ditch, effectively hidden from view unless someone thought he had hit a deer there the night before. The distraught young pilot called the Sacramento police."

Leah paused. Nye had gone very quiet and Rose was grim.

"June Lefcourt vouched for Booker. She said he was stone sober when he brought the furniture over for her and he never mentioned hitting anything. SPD did a blood alcohol on him that morning, but he was oh-oh by that time. There was no evidence of drunk driving, only reconstructive evidence about the speeding, and he had a good story about being uncertain what had happened because there weren't any streetlights on the slough road."

Rose turned to Nye, who sat rigid and stony. "It's got to be a coincidence, Ter. Some other day, got to be."

"So SPD," Leah continued, wondering what was happening, "didn't have much of a choice. They tried arresting Booker for vehicular homicide. But it couldn't stick. We charged him with reckless driving and his defense attorney, Judge Roche, got him a fine. June Lefcourt was his alibi. But he had to be under the influence when he ran into Johnson. Nobody sober hits a deer or a human being and just drives away unless they're too drunk or too scared." She took the file from Nye. "June played being his alibi for a vehicular homicide into being his wife, then into whatever else she wanted from him."

"Until he started with Drucker," Nye muttered. "Come on, Rosie. Let's go find these bastards." He lurched to his feet.

"What's going on?" Leah asked, her phone imperiously demanding attention.

"I'll tell you later," Rose said, following after the rapidly moving Nye.

Leah reached for the phone, perplexed. It was very hard to understand cops sometimes. They reacted strangely to some things, sentimental about cars and certain people, callously amused at suffering. Or so it seemed.

I don't know what's going on in Nye's head, she realized. Maybe he's too sensitive because he's an old cop and everything's pregnant with memories.

June Booker came out of the governor's office on the arm of the governor's chief of staff. The phalanx of cameras and tourists, spectators, and people who had walked over from the rotunda gave her a solemn round of applause. The chief of staff patted her arm and kissed her cheek. Several people tried to talk to her, but burly CHP officers pushed them back.

Cooper came forward. "I'll get Mrs. Booker to her car," he

said to the CHP officers, all of whom he knew. They offered to help, but he insisted, holding June Booker's firm arm tightly. She was silent.

He took her down the marble corridor into the Department of Finance near the entrance to the capitol, pushing by startled analysts and secretaries, and brought her into the small, always chilly conference room just inside the railing that kept the public back.

He shut the door. She regarded him clinically. She had a waxy fixed look, but her eyes darted to him and around the room. She touched her mouth. She was dressed for fashionable public mourning, silver jewelry, expensive night-black suit. She looked around at the cushioned prison-made chairs and carefully sat down.

"I didn't think you were being gallant, Mr. *Cooper?*" she asked. "We haven't met but I know Joyce Gutherie very well. She and Jerry were good friends."

"This is an official meeting," he said, impressed by her bold casualness. He almost hesitated. Talking to her without witnesses was outside procedure and common sense. But too much was happening. And too many incidents were starting to bubble up in Sacramento and around the nation. They were running out the clock.

"Well, in that case, you might like to factor in that the governor has just decided to call a special election to fill Jerry's seat in Congress at the earliest possible date. I'll have to give it very deep thought, but I'm *inclined* to run myself." She smiled at him, a warm and otherwise convincing smile. "I can carry on Jerry's work. He would have wanted that, I know."

Along the plain walls were standard framed photos of California scenes, beaches and palms, desert and mountains, freeways glittering at night. Cooper thought of June Booker representing California in Congress. He didn't think it would happen.

"Mrs. Booker, you're not going to run for anything."

"Really?"

"Sandy Drucker was murdered last night. She was tortured

before she died, apparently to make her reveal something."

He watched the satisfaction, triumph, and gloating that flickered across June Booker's face and then vanished back into the carefully maintained neutral public expression. "I'm *very* sorry to hear that. She was—" June Booker chuckled abruptly. "I'm not sorry. No. And it sounds like it was very painful. No. Somehow"—she chuckled again— "that makes it much better."

"Both the FBI and the district attorney will be opening public investigations into the money that your husband illegally accepted, Mrs. Booker. You also took money. That's why you're not leaving Sacramento. You'll be lucky to stay out of prison."

He had never, in his time as a prosecutor, fallen to posturing and empty threats. He didn't know if he could put together enough of a case to convict June Booker, but it was intolerable, after seeing Sandy Drucker's awful fear the night before and how she was killed, to let this gloating go on any longer.

"I have a lot of lawyers, Mr. Cooper," she said, getting up, adjusting her skirt carefully. "I think I can stand whatever you're planning."

"Your husband told you he was letting the FBI secretly record meetings with other members of Congress. He told you he was going to prison himself."

She frowned theatrically as if what he said was surprising. "Jerry was a complex man, full of contradictions. He liked to live well and liked to feel guilty about it. He loved me and he had his whore too. He called me just before he made his speech and he told me all about his other life with the FBI, how they had him in a straitjacket. He had to cooperate to get a lighter sentence. And, *oh by the way,*" she snarled, "he said he was leaving me for the whore."

"Who did you tell?"

"There's only one man I know who has the courage to take charge of out-of-hand situations. I contacted Ralph right away. He suggested buying the whore off, but the whore wouldn't be bought." She laughed unpleasantly. "Isn't that a remarkable inconsistency?"

"Payton hired the Russian to kill Jerry?"

"What *Russian?* Ralph doesn't know any *Russians* as far as I know and he certainly wouldn't have killed Jerry. He's not a murderer, Mr. Cooper."

"Who killed your husband?"

"I don't have any idea. I didn't. Ralph didn't. I suppose the TV is right and it was terrorists. Or. . ." She paused with polished theatricality. "We could all be thankful for some very bad luck coming Jerry's way."

"I'm going to arrest you soon, Mrs. Booker," Cooper vowed.

"When you try, you'll put Joyce Gutherie out of a job. Yourself too, I assume." She moved past him. "I'm going home to consider my candidacy announcement, perhaps talk to Ralph about timing and message. I'll have to break the news to him about the whore. He'll feel as miserable as I do."

Cooper tried for a moment to imagine what Jerry Booker's life since the accident on the slough road had been, the hours and days with June turning into years. The reckless wartime heroics that got him the medals were only missed chances to get out of the trap by dying. And just when darkness must have seemed to crowd around him entirely and forever, he met Sandy Drucker. For a little while, he saw the light, even if it meant going to prison. Then someone stepped from an alley and it all ended. For all of them, June, Payton, Manzoni, because Cooper could not admit any one of them would benefit from Booker's final descent into darkness.

No one wanted to atone for that drunken accident more than Jerry Booker, Cooper thought.

"Good-bye, Mrs. Booker," he said brusquely. "I'd get all the lawyers you can. You're going to need them."

She seemed genuinely confused. "A *Russian?*"

"Don't bother, Rosie," Nye said, speeding faster along Highway 160, cars honking at him as he changed lanes. "I had him that day. I could've busted him and he wouldn't have killed that kid.

What am I saying? None of this would've happened. Oh, man," he said again with self-contempt.

"How were you supposed to know he'd keep drinking? You read minds?"

"Look, even then, I had a pretty good insider's perspective on the habits of drunks. Booker was going to keep drinking until he passed out. Or started driving."

"So slow down now," she ordered. "I'd like to get to Payton in one piece."

Nye nodded forlornly. "Twenty years' worth of dominoes all falling down. I'm going back to church."

"Don't make fun," she warned. She, Luis, and Annorina were regular communicants at a small Catholic church three blocks from their home. "Ter, accept it. It's long gone. You made a call and it's done."

"Think so? I knew a rook, he almost got bounced out of the department on a bad call about a woman he was dating." He waved a free hand. "The point is, he managed to stay on the job. Ten years later, he spends all his free time looking for a missing baby a crackhead mom left some place. He finds the kid, saves its life. He got bounced from the department, that kid would've died because he wasn't there to save him."

"I heard it," she said. "I heard all of your war stories."

"You ain't heard all of them."

"What're you saving them for, old man?" she said, pleased she had gotten him off his latest canter down morose memory lane.

Rose's personal cell phone again chirped demandingly in her jacket pocket. Twice she had involuntarily reached for it. "I will not answer," she said. "Luis's got to take care of things right now." Their radio sounded. It was Drier putting out a call for anyone in the vicinity. Two homicides and a man with a gun. Nye hit the lights and the siren, searching for the nearest off-ramp he could take to head for Drier's location.

"He found the Russian," Rose said.

"Yeah," Nye said. "But I had him that day. I had him."

Drier had a year-round tan that made him look like an apricot roll, Rose once told Nye. They met him and eight other SPD officers outside a small lemon-yellow bungalow off Alhambra Boulevard, within sight of the Sacramento Blood Bank and an enormous green water storage tank. It was a neighborhood of Hispanics and new immigrants, and people were outside their homes warily and curiously keeping an eye on the police now thronging the narrow tree-shaded street.

"You think I should let the FBI guys know what we got here?" Drier asked without leaving any doubt how he felt personally.

"Hell no," Nye responded. "We did the work, we make the catch," and Rose nodded.

Drier was satisfied. "Okay, come on inside for a second. I got three sets of our guys checking the area. Couple of neighbors saw this puke heading west"—he pointed down the street—"on foot about ten minutes ago. No weapon anybody saw, but I bet he's got it."

"Show us what you got," Rose said, already heading to the bungalow.

It was tight and stuffy inside, a maze of rent-to-own plastic and bulky furniture and a large-screen TV. The crime scene van techs hadn't even arrived yet to process the interior. Drier was very pleased how fast he'd assembled enough cops to sweep the nearby streets for their suspect.

The small bedroom had a single narrow bed, more furniture crammed into it than it could realistically accommodate. Nye surveyed the bodies together as Rose took a swift look at each. The woman, naked and contorted, lay half off the bed, three bloody bullet wounds in her back. She had been trying to scramble from the bed. The man, also naked, lay on his back, eyes closed, his face red-sheathed.

"Bastard got it while he was sleeping." Nye looked around. "I'm figuring she's Mrs. Kokoshkin. Who's the boyfriend?"

Drier pointed at the clothes neatly folded on a brown-upholstered chair. "I looked in his wallet there. Leonid Vaiskopf. Works downtown for an architect."

Rose looked at the shirt, pants, and shoes. "Pretty expensive."

Drier nodded. "He lives downtown too, 1820 N Street."

Nye mirthlessly chuckled. "Same place as Booker's lady." He peered at the eternally frozen faces on the bed. "I guess, what? Twelve hours maybe? Something like that? Kokoshkin nails both of them yesterday, like around five or six, depending on how long it took him to get from 1820 N back here."

"Your wits say he started walking a few minutes ago?" Rose asked Drier.

"Yeah, he came out of the house like he's high, stoned, they said."

Nye had an instant dark image bloom in his mind. He was still grappling with the revelation about his own chance meeting with Jerry Booker. "This is nasty. This guy stayed with these two all night after he shot them."

Rose's phone went off and she ignored it again. "So the husband goes looking for his wife and her boyfriend at the boyfriend's fancy condo. He doesn't find them. He's leaving just as Congressman Booker gets out of the cab."

Drier frowned. "You think? Why'd the Russian shoot Booker?"

Nye carefully stepped back to the door. "Kokoshkin was pissed. He was going to kill his wife and this mope." He pointed at the bed. "Then they ain't around and he's leaving and there's Booker right in front of him." Nye looked at Rose. "He shot the first people he saw, Booker and the cabdriver."

"Maybe he saw Booker on TV," Rose said with a sad nod. "Kokoshkin maybe just saw the congressman's speech."

"We got to find this guy," Nye said. "He's still pissed and he's still got a gun."

Nye and Rose worked with Drier to seal off the neighborhood and organize a grid pattern search of the streets and backyards. They discreetly put out a call for more cops, only highlighting that the suspect was armed and on foot without suggesting who it was.

Fifteen minutes later, Rose spotted a prematurely balding young man in a blue Raley's Supermarket nylon jacket. He was sitting on the curb and he had a .38 limply in his hands. He shook his head slowly back and forth as if listening to something unpleasant and he was muttering a woman's name.

Rose quickly and very carefully radioed Drier and the other cops. She and Nye had slowly taken out their department-issued Glocks.

"Mike?" Nye called out casually but firmly. "Mike Kokoshkin? Is that you, Mike?"

The young man raised his eyes, the gun in his hands pointed down at the asphalt.

"Mr. Kokoshkin," Rose said now that Nye had his attention without alarming him, "put down the gun and put your hands behind your head and lie facedown. Do it right now."

They had moved to the protection of trees across the street from Kokoshkin. He loudly called out in Russian and then a woman's name again. He did not let go of the .38.

"Put the gun down now!" Rose snapped commandingly.

Nye flashed on the horrific possibility that they were being drawn into a suicide by cop. But he didn't fire yet.

He didn't have to. Neither did Rose. As she ordered Kokoshkin a final time, he screamed a woman's name twice, jammed the .38's muzzle into his mouth, and blew the back of his head off.

Cooper sat at his desk, Leah opposite him in a cracked leather chair after she pushed several paperbound California Supreme Court reports to the floor. They had been picking at a tasteless lunch, both anxious not to spend much time eating. The half-empty cartons cooled as Cooper spoke to Walker on the speakerphone.

"I can repeat it again if you'd like, Agent Walker. We're expediting the ballistics examination of the .38, but you and I can make a safe assumption right now that it's the weapon that killed Booker and Lorenz."

Leah stood up. "There's no question Kokoshkin didn't kill Sandy Drucker. We've got several witnesses who saw him come home last night, probably right after he'd killed the congressman. He presumably found his wife and her boyfriend together, killed them, and then didn't come out again until about thirty minutes ago."

"At which time," Cooper said, "he shot himself."

"The investigation's wide open," Walker said, his voice crackling as his cell phone cut in and out. "I've still got Drucker's killer outstanding. I'm bringing Manzoni and Payton in. You can tackle Booker's wife, Cooper." It was a taunt.

Leah crossed her arms. June Booker had complained quickly and loudly to powerful people in Washington about Denny's impromptu interview with her. "We'll be happy to," she said to Walker.

She smiled at Denny. They hadn't told Walker that Nye and Tafoya were on their way to pick up Ralph Payton and another set of SPD detectives were already questioning Manzoni in an interview room. But there was another reason for this urgent call. The president had gone on national TV within the last hour, appealing for calm and resolution and tolerance. "It's getting out of hand," Cooper had said as they watched. "He knows it and he doesn't have a way to stop it."

Then the news about Kokoshkin came through.

"Agent Walker," Cooper said, hunching forward to the phone, "you and I've got to make a call right now. We need to let the attorney general know Booker wasn't killed by terrorists. We've got to get that word out immediately."

"I don't have Drucker's killer yet."

"We can't wait," Cooper said sharply. "Either you call the AG or I do. If I do, I will make it very clear you're obstructing justice."

Leah gave him a silent high sign.

"Agent Walker," Cooper pressed relentlessly, "it's over."

EIGHTEEN

"HOW DO YOU WANT TO GO IN?" Rose asked Nye as they parked in the driveway of Ralph Payton's riverfront house.

"Front door. You take the back in case he runs," Nye said, getting out of the car and checking his gun quickly.

"Heck no, old man. You take the back. He runs, you go after him," she said. He knew she was joking. Civilians like Payton, assuming they tried to flee, usually headed for front doors for some reason. It must seem like a natural exit.

Nye nodded. "Okay, I'll be around back. We could wait for more backup."

"We got him," Rose said confidently. "We wait any longer, the FBI's going to grab him."

"It's not a rib, Rosie. Just offering."

They both fell silent. On the way to the large sprawling colonial home behind a salmon-pink sandstone wall, she and Nye had debated Kokoshkin's suicide and who had killed Sandy Drucker. The soft Payton didn't seem right, but that was not dispositive. Manzoni was younger and more likely. June Booker was likely, too.

"Either way," Nye said, "we take Payton very carefully."

He waited as Rose moved into position at the front door. She would knock and announce herself after a count of thirty to give him time to get to the back of the house.

He paused for a moment and saw Rose observing him. A sleek avocado-colored 1958 Jaguar was pulled up to the side of the house on the gravel driveway. The engine was running quietly, the driver-side door open. Nye peered in quickly. A hand-tooled leather briefcase lay on the passenger seat. Above it were dark red spots on the leather upholstery and the carpeting was torn, as if frantic, agony-driven kicks had aimed at it repeatedly. The cigarette lighter was missing. Nye thought that Payton could have dropped it or lost it while he burned Sandy Drucker as she lay tied on the seat beside him. Maybe he threw it out the window afterward. Nye's face set in a cold, iron mask.

He strode silently across the gravel, his Glock out. The carefully manicured lawn to his right ended at the river's edge. At the dock on the dark autumn-chilled water rode a twenty-foot-long alabaster-white and mint-green boat, perfect for long summer days on the river entertaining clients, sipping endless drinks. On the boat's stern was its name in curled script: PAYTON'S PAYOFF.

He moved noiselessly and alertly to the patio doors that led out to the lawn and the boat and escape.

Rose counted slowly and methodically, her gun drawn. She felt her heart beating heavily, as if she had run two miles around the Sac State track. The violence of Kokoshkin's suicide had unsettled her. It was the first time she had ever seen someone shot and the first time she had seen someone die.

"Mr. Payton," she called out firmly in a clear and steady voice. "This is the Sacramento police. I'm Detective Tafoya. Open the door."

She knocked on the door hard and hit the bell and repeated her announcement. It was required by law before what she did next. She tried the brass door handle, twisted it hard, and kicked the door open instantly.

Rose's heart was hitting the side of her chest almost painfully. She was glad Terry couldn't see her. I've got to look like I'm scared shitless, she thought.

The foyer was wide and white-tiled, the early afternoon sun shining through large windows just beyond in the dining room. She listened intently. She didn't hear anything. She moved very carefully and silently toward the dining room, then next to the kitchen, making certain each space was clear. In a few moments, Rose knew she would meet Terry coming in from the back of the house and they would search for Payton room by room.

He had to be nearby. The car's outside, engine's going, he's boogying, she thought. Her cell phone abruptly chirped and she reflexively dropped her free hand to it.

Payton appeared from the nearest corner of the dining room. He had a black, small gun pointed at her. Rose saw him, the gun, the sunlight behind him that illuminated her so well.

Payton fired three times.

Nye heard the small-caliber shots and started running. He slammed open the glass patio doors. "Rose!" he yelled. "Rose! Rose!"

A part of his mind cataloged the sounds of the shots. Could be more than a .22 but probably wasn't. The confined space of the house made the discharge falsely resonate, but the shots were definitely small caliber. Like the gun that killed Drucker.

He was still moving at a run when he almost collided with Payton. Payton's face was beet red, sweat-streaked, his hair disheveled. "Christ," he stammered with a fear-tinged drawl. "I heard gunshots back there," and he pointed behind him.

"Get the fuck down on the floor now!" Nye shouted, his gun aimed at Payton's torso.

"Oh my God, oh my God," Payton stammered again, lunging as if to fall to the plush turquoise carpeting. With unexpected athleticism, he stopped and moved his hands, scrabbling for something in his sport coat pocket.

Nye shot him twice and then once again. The impact of the three bullets twisted Payton around and he fell face forward, his right hand jammed into his sport coat pocket. "Rose!" Nye shouted desperately again. He kicked Payton's hand from the pocket and ripped it open and kicked again at the black .22, spinning it under a glass-topped coffee table. Overhead, a teak-wood-bladed fan continued to turn lazily and obliviously.

Nye bent to Payton's neck, a rage he hadn't felt for years washing through him like a red-hot tide. There was no pulse.

He automatically grabbed the .22 from under the coffee table because you don't leave weapons lying around if you think a suspect can get at it. Like that rookie who let an angry couple get hold of his baton and beat his partner.

Nye felt enveloped in his rage and desperation. He gasped, as if he couldn't breathe.

He found Rose on her back, gun arm extended uselessly on the white-tiled foyer floor almost to the kitchen. He was on his knees beside her, letting go of the .22 and his own gun, calling her name with something like the intensity of the man he and Rose had seen only an hour before. There was little blood. Her eyes were wide and unfocused.

Shot twice, one missed her, he thought calmly, even as his hand groped for his radio to call for help and he heard someone shouting wildly.

It's me, he realized.

Cooper lowered his head so he could see into the Rolls Royce's interior. CHP officers were impatiently waving cars forward as traffic on the busy highway slowed to see what was happening.

Behind the Rolls, SPD officers were talking to three motor-ists, their cars pulled to the side of the highway. They pointed and the officers wrote down what they said. It was a very fresh crime scene.

"Everybody saw it," said the SPD sergeant who obligingly acted as tour guide for Cooper. "Jag and this car pull over. Driver, white male, gets out of the Jag, gets into the Rolls. He gets out, he drives away. The Rolls stays here."

Cooper nodded absentmindedly. He had been tired yesterday, but now, with everything swiftly shifting and changing, he was somehow refreshed. It was paradoxical.

"Who found her?" he asked the sergeant.

"Guy and his wife back there." He gestured at one set of motorists. "They thought she was sleeping or needed help. Then they saw her."

Cooper straightened up. CHP helicopters were swooping in above them to monitor the highway. He glanced at June Booker a final time. Her head was thrown back, mouth and eyes open, seeming to gape in astonishment. The cluster of .22 wounds to her head was nearly unnoticeable. "I told her she wasn't going to run for anything," he said over the traffic's rumble and hiss.

"Hey," the sergeant asked solemnly, "is it true we got an officer down?"

Cooper nodded. "I'm going to the hospital now," he said, turning to his own car.

The throng of reporters and the curious, and law enforcement officers from all over the area and more coming had turned South Sacramento Community Hospital instantly into an attraction, like a pilgrim's destination.

The Intensive Care Unit on the third floor where Rose lay was guarded tightly, the nurses and doctors incredulous and annoyed at the commotion around them.

Nye stood at the rear of a densely crowded small auditorium on the first floor. Cooper and Gutierrez stood in front of the massed reporters and cameras. Nye was detached, thinking of Rose upstairs.

"Let me repeat this one more time," Cooper said calmly. "Congressman Booker and Jaime Lorenz were killed by a single deranged individual who committed suicide earlier this morning as he was about to be apprehended. This individual also murdered his wife and another man. There is no evidence of any other groups or individuals involved in either of these sets of crimes. I am informed by Special Agent Walker of the FBI's Sacramento office that we can expect a similar statement to be issued by the attorney general in a matter of minutes."

"What about Booker's wife? Who killed her?" a reporter hoarsely called out.

"June Booker's murder is still being investigated by the very capable members of Chief Gutierrez's department." Cooper nodded to the stolid Gutierrez, who looked tired and pleased to have some resolution so quickly. "I'm sure he will be forthcoming with any information as soon as he can."

Gutierrez bobbed his head. "We are on top of the investigation."

There were more questions and more details, and Cooper and the chief stayed to answer them for another half hour. But, Nye thought, it doesn't change anything.

He had more important things to do.

"I think you should think about some other location, Agent Walker," Cooper said. Leah blew on a paper cup of tea. "I don't anticipate you're going to get much cooperation in the future from local law enforcement."

Walker watched the reporters moving their cameras to do remotes about the press conference. "Funny you mentioned that," he said. "I don't think Sacramento's going to work out either. Chang wants me to head up an anti-corruption task force, so I'll be heading to Washington for a little while, get it set up, and then we'll hit the road."

"A very good idea. You can try to net some of the people Booker reeled in."

"Maybe. There's a lot of bad guys. The task force might just start fresh."

"I wish you luck."

"Sure."

"No, I do," Cooper said. "Nobody benefits from public corruption."

Walker gave Leah a half salute and headed away with Zilaff and his band of agents.

"I thought I saw Nye." Leah finished the tea. "He looks rocky."

"He was upstairs with Tafoya's family last time I saw him." Cooper scanned the moving swirl of faces in the auditorium. "Do you want to stop by again before we go?"

She shook her head. "No. We can come back tomorrow." She tossed the cup into a metal trash container. "Are you really going to call Joyce?"

"I have to. If she wants my resignation, she's entitled to it. I didn't handle things well. Walker made his mistakes, but I did too."

"She won't take it, Denny."

They walked toward the chaotic lobby and the even more chaotic parking lot.

"She might." He looked at Leah. "I think you want my job."

"I do not," she said, but she made certain he heard the insincerity in her tone. "Believe me."

"I suppose the competition will keep things interesting," and he touched her hand.

━━━

Nye still didn't like Luis Tafoya even under these circumstances. The man was always avoiding his eyes, and he seemed anxious to get away from the hospital. Annorina, dark eyes wide and fearful, clutched her father's arm or clung to him.

"Any time," Nye said again, "you need anything, Luis, you

call me. Day or night, you call." He gave Rose's husband a card again. *I think this is the third one in the last couple of hours,* and he realized it must make him seem confused. He was anything but confused. He was clear about what he needed to be doing.

"All right, Terry," Luis Tafoya said. "Maybe I call you for sure." He was a short man, slender, and dressed in bright colors. "Rose always says you're the best."

"See, what does she know?" He laughed and patted Annorina. "Hey, I got a daughter too, you know? I ever tell you?"

Annorina shook her head. They had been together at picnics and a few department bowling nights, but the conversation had been awkward with Rose and Luis together.

"My daughter called me a little while ago," Nye said. "She saw me on TV and we had a good talk, first time in a while. I told her, your mom is going to be okay. I wouldn't tell my own daughter that if it wasn't true. So you believe me."

Luis hugged her. "We going in to see her for a while, Terry."

"Yeah, you go. I got to get back downtown. I'm going to a desk job until they get the shooting sorted out. It's standard. I mean, this is the first one in twenty-plus years for me, but I ain't worried. It's just standard procedure."

He didn't tell Luis or Annorina that he had given up his Glock for testing as part of the administrative process that would determine whether he had justifiably shot Ralph Payton. But he truly was not concerned. It did not matter to him.

He waved to Annorina. He gravely shook Luis's small hand and told him that they would be in touch later that day.

He pretended to leave. Instead, he went to the cafeteria on the second floor because it had a wide window that overlooked the hospital's entire parking lot. Nye got a cup of coffee and found an empty Formica-topped table near the window. He checked his watch and pushed the coffee cup slowly back and forth in front of him. People came and went from the cafeteria and he tensed only when a group of laughing, loudly braying reporters came in, grabbed packages of snacks, paid, and left. They hadn't spotted him.

Ninety minutes later, he saw Luis Tafoya and Annorina, her

hands holding her father as he tried to get his car keys, come out and get into their car. Nye waited until he was sure they had driven away.

He went up to the third floor. At the nurse's station for the ICU, a bank of TV monitors and readouts showed the status of the twenty patients who lay in falsely serene silence. The nurse on duty, stout and imperious, tried to stop him from going farther. He showed her his badge. "Police business. It's not going to take long."

The badge might have convinced her to let him through, but it was the implacable determination in how he glared at her that made her relent.

Nye went immediately to the fifth bed. Rose lay swaddled in the embrace of tubes and wires and machines around her that clicked, hummed, and blinked. He found a metal-backed chair and slid it up to the bed. This was the first time he had seen her alone since the shooting. Her hair was bunched beneath her head, and her mouth was half open and a breathing tube in her throat was taped to her chin.

"Hello again, Rosie," he said with joviality, sitting down. He took off his coat and hung it carefully on the back of the chair. "I bet you feel like crap. Don't worry. You can tell me all about it, much as you like, when they get this stuff out of your mouth and we can talk."

Her eyes flickered. She hears me, he thought. I know that.

"So. I got Luis all set up, he'll call me and I'll help out whatever he needs. The kid's going to be okay. I'll keep an eye on her."

Rose's eyes opened and she looked over at him without moving her head.

"So I'll bring you up on everything." He snorted. "What a goddamn circus. You should see everybody. Kind of disappointed Booker got blown away by a whack job and not terrorists. He's still going out a hero. Walker's boss lost interest in making news about a dead congressman's bad habits."

He thought he saw Rose try to smile through the breathing tube.

Without thinking about it, he reached over and lightly took her dry, warm hand where it lay motionless.

"Okay, we got some time here. I'm going to take advantage of this deal." He grinned over at her, like they were in the car, heading out on a call. "Because I do have a couple war stories you haven't heard. Maybe"—he raised his eyebrows menacingly—"a couple you heard already, you are going to hear again."

He cleared his throat. Her hand didn't move in his, but that was fine. She would be fine, too.

"Here's one I never told you. This goes way back. We had this after-hours bar, dealing all kinds of crap inside, and I got the DA to let me get a tow truck and a chain and pull the front door off. Except the whole front came off," he said, and the sound of his voice happily talking to her was the only human sound, the only comforting and redeeming sound around them.

It was enough.

ABOUT THE AUTHOR

WILLIAM P. WOOD is the bestselling author of nine novels and one nonfiction book. As a deputy district attorney in California, he handled thousands of criminal cases and put on over 50 jury trials. Two of Wood's novels have been produced as motion pictures, including *Rampage*, filmed by Academy Award–winning director William Friedkin (*The French Connection, The Exorcist, Rules of Engagement*), and *Broken Trust*, filmed by Jane Fonda Films with the screenplay by Joan Didion and John Gregory Dunne. Wood's books have been translated into several foreign languages. He lives in Sacramento, California.

CPSIA information can be obtained
at www.ICGtesting.com
Printed in the USA
JSHW030329260720
6863JS00003B/165